ISLAND
escape

VIV DANIELS

WORD *for* WORD

Island Escape

Copyright © 2015 by Viv Daniels

Cover design © Vania Stoyanova
Cover photo © Vania Stoyanova
Cover photo © depositphotos@york_76

Published by Word for Word
ISBN: 978-1-937135-15-7

For princesses, farm boys,
and everyone who loves them

one

June 25, 1989

KALINA ST. CLAIRE TUGGED her bikini top into place, squared her shoulders, and marched out of the stateroom and onto the sun-drenched deck. Everything glowed, even through the mirrored lenses of her sunglasses. The deck of Bradley's father's yacht was made of gleaming wood instead of blinding white fiberglass, but the South Pacific sun bounced off every metal rail and boom and winch with a cruel sort of sparkle.

She knew the deckhands were paid to keep things clean, but did they have to scrub everything until it shimmered? Even the wet wood seemed brighter than it had any right to.

"Look who's showing her face!" called her friend Lisa, lounging on a deck chair with some trashy novel. Lisa checked the watch lying on her towel. "And it's only two o'clock."

"Local time?" Kalina replied. "I'm still on LA time."

"It's six p.m. in LA, hon," said Tiffany, who occupied the lounge chair to Lisa's left. "It gets later going east."

"London," said Kalina. "I meant London." She'd been in London only last month, then Paris, Monaco, Morocco, the Seychelles, Hong Kong… who gave a shit what actual time zone she was in? Everywhere she was had the same schedule — party all night, sleep all day, check out the beaches or the shops or the clubs if she was up for it. The last time she'd kept track of her hours was during her first attempt at freshman year in college, and that was…

The boat hit a wave and Kalina shot out her hand for balance as the hammer inside her skull grew insistent. "Please tell me it's vodka-tonic-thirty."

"Tough luck again, sweet pea," said Lisa. Her parents were some kind of Texas oil magnates, and occasionally the country came out of her. "There was a mix-up with the service schedule. We're on our own at the bar this afternoon."

Tiffany glared at her and Lisa fell silent.

Kalina swallowed back a throat full of bile and crossed to the outdoor bar. Glass, check. Ice cubes, check. Vodka… as she reached for the bottle, she saw a half-finished vial of coke that must have somehow slipped behind the bar.

Even better.

The stopper was shaped like a little snowflake, which was probably someone's idea of a hilarious joke.

Kalina drew out a line on the glass serving tray and grabbed a cocktail straw. A little bump was all she needed this afternoon.

She sighed as the coke whizzed through her sinuses and muffled the hammer. Ahh. Who needed vodka when you had cocaine? Okay, time to get the party started. Kalina and her girls needed bellinis. She rooted through the bar fridge for champagne and peach nectar, mixed up a pitcher and joined the girls back at the lounge chairs with a tangle of stemware clutched between her fingers.

"Where is everyone?" she asked as she started pouring drinks. Lisa demurred — a lifetime of Southern cooking had left her with a tendency toward a fat ass — but Tiffany took a drink, and so did Mirelle and Stevie, who had just joined them on the deck, their hair wet from a jet ski ride.

"Tim and Jorge are downstairs in the video room with the Nintendo," Lisa explained, "and Decker and Bran are off the stern fishing."

"Great." Kalina took a slug from her champagne flute and smiled as the sweet bellini slid down her throat. She should probably eat something too, but lunch was over and she wasn't ready to venture into the kitchen alone. Not if the staff was still grumbling about *service schedule mix-ups*.

Kalina's friends might not know the truth, but the staff always did, especially on yachts this small. And the only service schedule mix-up was that one little bitch maid picked the wrong time to schedule a *service* on Kalina's boyfriend.

The room had been dark when Kalina entered, and she fumbled for the brass light switch. But when the light flickered on, she wasn't sure what she was looking at.

Bran sat on the bed, spread-eagled, his board shorts dangling awkwardly from one ankle, his head lolling back on his neck. And that cute, blonde stewardess, Anna, knelt before him, the khaki skirt of her uniform riding up over her lacy panties, her head buried in his crotch.

Kalina hardly knew what she was doing before she had a handful of that witch's blonde hair in her fist. "Get off him, you whore!" she'd shrieked, dragging the girl back as she yelped. Bran's dick flopped out of her mouth.

"Kalina?" Bran's eyes shot open. "I thought you were downstairs watching the movie."

"Are you cheating on me?" Kalina had screamed, as the girl slapped at her wrist until she let go. Anna whimpered and shied away, tugging her skirt down and the white flaps of her blouse closed over her exposed tits. "With this trash?"

"Oh my God," was all Bran had said.

"I want her off this boat," she said, staring down her nose at the little slut. "She's fired."

"What?" Anna cried. "You can't fire me. Bran's father is the one who owns—"

"Shut up," Kalina snapped. "No one is speaking to you."

"Kiki, honey…"

Ugh, she hated when he called her that. "I never want to see this tramp again. Do you hear?" She whirled on her heel and stomped out of their cabin.

Stupid Bran Nesbit and his stupid inability to keep his stupid cock in his stupid pants. Didn't he understand that half the girls he met would take a lot of Nesbit dick for even a scrap of the Nesbit fortune?

4

A diamond tennis bracelet, a trip on the helicopter—anything would do. He was trapped in a sea of gold-digging sluts.

Kalina knew well how this worked. Since the time she was fourteen, she'd been on the receiving end of the same treatment. Debonair older men trying to take control of the purse strings; hot, young gigolos hoping to get their greasy hands on her family money—it was disgusting. They gave her the full court press and then they vanished into thin air when they weren't instantly showered in gold. At least if she stuck with other rich kids, she knew they weren't in it for the cash.

She and Bran made a simple sort of sense, as long as he could follow basic ground rules. No outside pussy where she could catch them, and on their bed on an eighty-foot yacht was definitely a place that she'd catch them. There was fooling around and then there was humiliation, and Kalina St. Claire was not interested in being humiliated.

She felt a crease forming between her eyes and rubbed it away with her knuckles. It wouldn't do to start getting wrinkles at the tender age of twenty-two. She threw back her head and downed the rest of her bellini.

"I ordered snacks," Stevie was saying now, securing her bleach-blonde hair into a high ponytail with a neon scrunchie. "It's a mess down there in the galley, though, so who knows when they'll be by."

"Bran really needs to get his staff in order," Lisa sniffed.

Tiffany cleared her throat and turned the page of her magazine. "It's so hard to find good help these days." She snickered.

"Apparently some girl packed up and left at the last port or something," Stevie went on with a shrug. "The blonde?"

"Good riddance," said Mirelle. "That girl was such a flirt. She used to bend over and flash her tits at Jorge whenever she got a chance."

"Come on," said Lisa. "They know what they get paid for around here. A little bit of T&A, a better tip. Am I right, Kalina?"

Kalina shrugged and lay face down on a lounger. Time for some tanning. She unclipped the back of her bikini top and smoothed her hair out of the way.

Stevie and Mirelle did the same, though Mirelle was already a smooth, deep brown thanks to the Greek side of her heritage. She was an Onassis on her mother's side, after all.

"Well," said Stevie, "down in the galley they're all real upset about it. They said they don't know how she's supposed to get home."

"Please," Kalina spat out in clipped tones. "She got paid for the summer. She has a passport and spare cash to buy a plane ticket." She turned her face back into her towel and squeezed her eyes shut. Didn't know how to get home? Couldn't she read the signs at the airport ticket counter? The slut was hardly destitute.

Stupid Bran. He should have bought her a ticket. He couldn't even fire that whore right.

A minute passed and her friends were still talking about the stewardess. Just great. There were nearly thirty crewmembers down below gossiping, and now the story was going to drift up to the passengers. If her friends were curious, all they'd have to do is ask one of the crew. She raised her head and opened her mouth to change the subject.

The galley door banged open and a crewmember emerged with a tray of food. He held it between two hands, like he'd never carried a tray of food in his life. It was possible he hadn't — this was one of the deckhands, who helped with the pool and jet skis and general upkeep of the yacht. His name was Adam, and Kalina knew there wasn't a girl on board who hadn't wasted more than a little time watching him work.

Hello, sailor.

Adam was tall, with dark hair cut shaggy, skin golden from the sun, and a slim physique that showed off all those muscles he got from running lines and carrying supplies. He didn't have that broad-shouldered bodybuilder shape like Stallone or Schwarzenegger, but Kalina had never liked the 'roid look anyway. The crew uniforms were cheesy — pleated khaki pants with green and yellow D-ring belts and starched, white, long-sleeved shirts with the Nesbit family crest on the pocket, but somehow Adam made them look like military whites.

He also had a reputation as a killjoy. He never took part in the poker games the boys liked to play with the crew, never looked hung over after port leave like other crew members, and wasn't even the type to give you a gentle good morning, which was just fine with Kalina. She liked servants to remember their place. And from the stormy expression on his face right now, Adam knew his place and was not happy to be playing waiter this afternoon.

"Where do you want it?" he asked Stevie.

"Oh, anywhere," she sing-songed, waving her hand vaguely in the direction of the low side table near their lounge. The deckhand bent to put the tray down and Stevie mimed squeezing his butt cheeks.

Mirelle laughed. Kalina rolled her eyes. What was with people and screwing the help these days?

"Oh, Adam?" Stevie rose on her elbows, which had the effect of revealing her nipples to the world. "Before you go, can you pass me that tanning oil?"

The deckhand grabbed the bottle of oil and turned. His eyes widened as he caught sight of Stevie's tits, then he raised his gaze to the horizon, his jaw tightly clenched.

The girls all laughed. "So, not a homo," Tiffany murmured under her breath.

"Here," he said, holding the bottle out blindly.

Stevie raised herself up a little more to grab the bottle from his fingers, her breasts swinging freely in the breeze. "Also… I hate to be all this trouble, but can you help me get my back? I hate to have an uneven tan."

She really was laying it on thick, wasn't she? A beat passed, and then Adam snatched the bottle back and crouched next to Stevie on the blanket. He shook a bit of oil into his palm, then slapped it on her back as if he was applying a fresh coat of stain to the deck.

"Mmmmmm," moaned Stevie, like she was getting some kind of professional massage. "You're so good with your hands, Adam."

His lips were a thin line, his eyes cold as stone beneath his furrowed brow. "All set." He wiped his hands on the corner of a towel and stood. "Do you need anything else?"

"Well," she said coyly, "you could do my front."

"I think you can reach." He tossed the bottle on the seat next to her.

"If I think of something, I'll call you," Stevie said sweetly.

Adam grabbed the empty tray and started back toward the galley. He paused over Kalina's towel, casting a black band of shadow across her body.

"Are you done with this?" Weird. Despite Stevie's teasing, she hadn't heard anything dark in his voice when he'd been speaking to her. But with Kalina, there was something in his tone, the brewing of some great storm.

Kalina raised her head far enough to see he was gesturing to the empty bellini pitcher and her stemware. She clutched her towel to her chest and reached for the champagne flute. "Yes. Thank you."

Their fingers touched as she passed it over, and their eyes met. For a moment, the fizz of snow and champagne died down in her brain as she looked into his eyes.

People shouldn't be allowed to have eyes like that. Eyes that looked right into you and saw every last little thing that was wrong with you. Every awful, cheap thing that all the wealth in the world couldn't erase. Kalina tried to breathe, but her lungs wouldn't inflate. She was pinned like a bug under his gaze. A low, dirty, helpless bug.

And then he was gone, the galley door swinging shut behind his admittedly nice ass. She let out a breath. The sun was bright again, and she was buzzed and rich and surrounded by her friends and everything was just freaking fine, thank you very much.

Just fine.

two

FIFTY-SIX MORE DAYS, and this would all be over. Adam Truman marched down the corridor and into the galley, where he dumped the serving tray unceremoniously into the rack by the door. "Anything else?"

Mario, the line cook, whistled through his teeth and went back to chopping vegetables. "All for now, man. Thanks for stepping in."

Adam turned on the nearest faucet and starting washing the remnants of the tanning oil off his hands. "No problem." It would have been even less of a problem had Mario needed him to debone a fish or peel a mountain of potatoes. Deck service sucked. But the *Palanquin* had strict service guidelines, and that included not appearing in front of the passengers in kitchen clothes. Deckhands like Adam wore public uniforms, so if there was a service shortage, he had to play waiter while Mario and the other three other kitchen workers currently on duty in the galley had to stay out of sight.

Fifty-six more days and he'd be done working for people who faint at the sight of a little flour on an apron. Done with people like this, hopefully forever.

It was ironic. Adam had spent the last three years in Annapolis thinking how off base his father's sermons about the dangerous, secular world were. His classmates at St. John's were fascinating, intelligent, hard-working people. Even his sophomore summer's employer, a legacy politician who'd founded a DC think tank, was interesting. He treated his yacht crew like a little political science seminar, and Adam and the other crew members had spent many evenings talking history and philosophy with him over card and billiard games in his recreation cabin. Adam had been prepared to write his father's words off as just one more fundamentalist lie.

Then he'd signed on to the *Palanquin*. The description made it seem like a dream job— ports all over the South Pacific, the chance to learn about the cultures and geography of the southern hemisphere. But the reality was closer to something out of his parents' nightmares. Every one of the seven deadly sins was on full display on this yacht, all the greed and lust and sloth and gluttony they'd spent their lives warning him about. He'd thought the passengers were just kids, like him, but they weren't like anyone he'd met, either back home on the ranch or in Annapolis. They were shallow and selfish and worst of all, cruel.

What had that girl wanted him to do? Caress her breasts in front of all her friends? How was that remotely a turn-on? She was very pretty — they were all very pretty, in that way that money makes you smooth and lean and shiny all over — but Stevie, topless, taunting him, her tanned breasts dangling

11

down over her towel... she didn't want *him*. All she wanted was control.

The back door to the galley banged open and in strutted two tanned layabouts in board shorts and mirrored sunglasses. The shorter one was Decker, a whiny hanger-on that the other passengers ridiculed behind his back. The taller one everyone called Bran, though Adam's employment contract had listed him under some long, stuffy sounding thing with Roman numerals after it. Bran was his boss. And he was the worst of the lot.

Between them, they carried a large fish, still flopping. "Look what we got!" Bran cried, and slammed the fish down on the worktable, upending a bowl of chopped parsley and knocking three spoons out of their rack.

"An excellent catch, sir," Mario responded, gathering up the spoons and chucking them underhand into the dishwashing sink. "Would you like me to show you how to debone it?"

"Nah, man. That shit's boring." He pounded Mario, hard, on the back. "You can do it. We'll have this with dinner."

"Of course, sir," Mario replied. "Any request as to preparation?"

"Just ask the chef when he gets in. Chef knows what I like." He sauntered off, Decker following in his wake.

After the door shut, Mario clucked his tongue, and then dumped the fish and the ruined parsley down the chute that led back out into the sea. "Get me some filets from the freezer," he called to one of the other kitchen workers. "We're having fish for dinner."

"What was wrong with that one?" Adam asked. He was hardly an expert at fish. They occasionally got catfish from the creek, back at the ranch.

"Cigua," said the kitchen worker, Bruno, as he came back with the filets. "Reef fish have got poison in 'em."

"And even if we could have made that fish," Mario added, "there wouldn't be enough for all eight of them, and that'll piss the boss off, too. But there's no point arguing, so I just say yes, sir, and then dump it when he's not looking."

Mario was nearing fifty. Adam imagined it must rankle a lot to call someone like Bran his boss. Though Bran was a good five or so years older than Adam's own twenty-two, he still acted like a child, throwing temper tantrums whenever he didn't get his way and acting like the world revolved around him.

"Are there any fish safe to eat around here?" Adam asked before he could stop himself. Funny, he'd been gone from home for years, but those survivalist instincts never quite died. Even out here, on a luxury yacht, he was trying to figure out how to live off the land. Or the ocean, in this case. Still… this area of the Pacific was full of islands and islanders who lived off seafood. He couldn't imagine them avoiding such an abundant food source.

"The fish could have been safe," Mario said. "And any island you go to the locals will tell you what's okay and what's not. Usually a smaller fish is better than a larger fish. But whatever the local rule is, I'm not about to put my job on the line. These kids get sick, it'll be my ass in a sling, not Prince Nesbit's."

The rest of the kitchen staff chuckled.

That part was certainly true. Look what had happened to poor Anna. The stewardess had appeared nice enough to Adam. Maybe even a little too nice, since she hadn't seemed quite so disgusted by Bran Nesbit as the rest of the crew. At least, she'd let him have sex with her.

And look how that had turned out. She'd done whatever he asked, and Bran had left her at the last port with barely enough money to cover her travel expenses home. The crew had all pitched in to wire her an extra check at the end of the summer, and had already arranged amongst them to include her in the customary gratuity split.

Though Adam was beginning to wonder if Bran and his friends would weasel out on the tip too. At this point, he didn't put much past them.

The passengers on this boat could do no wrong. Their lives were consequence-free, as far as Adam could tell. None of them had employment, very few had even tried college, and they all carried around large amounts of illegal drugs everywhere they went. But no one ever bothered them, and they didn't seem worried about anything… other than pissing off their parents and getting cut out of the will.

Fifty-six more days.

Mario glanced down at the call board. "Another order. Pizza bites." He scowled. "For this I went to a culinary academy." He grabbed a box of packaged goodies out of the freezer and popped a dish in the microwave. "Stick around, amigo."

Adam nodded. Pizza bites he could microwave himself. Yet he appreciated how Mario spent time arranging them on a china plate, garnishing them with fresh chopped parsley and an orchid sprig.

"You make these look gourmet, Mario."

"Anything worth doing is worth doing well," the line cook replied. "Even making garbage for rich assholes."

Now there was a sentiment Adam could agree with. He may hate working on the *Palanquin*, but he was still going to do an irreproachable job. He needed the money for his final year at St. John's. So he'd ignore the boys' invitations to lose his wages back to them at their nightly poker games, and the girls' invitations to be their boy toy. Sure, they were beautiful, but there was an ugliness inside them that Adam recoiled from, like fruit gone rotten at the core.

He'd do his job, no more, no less. Just fifty-six more days of keeping his head down and his mouth shut and he would never have to see any of these people ever again. Adam retrieved his tray, placed the dish of goodies in the center, and headed out to the video room.

Yes, sir. Very good, sir. Your wish is my command, sir.

All four of the male passengers were seated in front of a large TV, playing video games. Empty beer bottles littered the surface of a nearby coffee table, along with a small mirror still dusted with specks of cocaine. Cigarette smoke hung heavy in the air.

"—Still shutting you out?" the one called Jorge was asking Bran. "What's her problem? You got rid of what's-her-tits."

Adam swallowed back his bile. *What's-her-tits?* Of course, they'd never remember Anna's name. They didn't know any of their names, though they'd all been living in close quarters for over a month. He skirted around the couch to place the tray on the coffee table. No one so much as looked up.

Is there anything else you need, sir? Of course, sir. As you wish, sir. Adam kept the chorus going in his head, drowning out anything else that might rise to the surface.

Bran's face was intent on the screen, his hands holding the controller jumping every time the little plumber bashed his head into a brick. "Yeah, well, nothing's good enough for Kalina St. Claire."

Right. The girlfriend. The one with the tousled hair and the dead eyes. The only one who had ever bothered to say thank you to him. Kalina was possibly the most attractive girl on the boat, or she would be if she ever got a decent night's sleep or a few sober hours in a row.

The one named Tim shook his head. "I dunno, dude. Is it worth the trouble?"

"It will be," Bran said, jabbing at the controller until the plumber figure hopped up and down on a turtle of some sort. Adam had never really gotten into video games. They hadn't been allowed back at the ranch, and when he'd gotten to college it seemed a waste of time to pretend to kill creatures on a screen when there was so much reading to be done.

"Yeah," echoed Decker. "When her grandfather kicks it."

The other three men didn't respond, and Decker lapsed into an awkward silence as Adam departed the room.

He'd never understand rich people. It was considered the height of rudeness for them to ever speak about money, but at the same time, every single one of their conversations centered on the topic. Each one of the young people on this yacht wore their fortunes like stones around their necks, their romantic and social interactions seemingly based on their financial standings. After working on the *Palanquin* for a month, Adam knew their scores too. Decker was low man on the totem pole, from a family with an important name, but with no real money of his own. Bran's father kept what Bran considered a tight leash on his allowance, and everyone on staff knew how much it rankled him that his trust fund was untouchable while his father still lived. Jorge was European royalty, and Tim's father was some kind of real estate mogul. The girl who'd flashed him up on deck, Stevie, came from Texas oil money, the black-haired one was a shipping heir, and Tiffany's parents were in banking.

And apparently Kalina's grandfather was the one holding her purse strings.

Every single one of these people defined by who their parents were, by what their parents did. And happy to live that way. Adam shuddered as he made his way back to crew quarters, deep in the bowels of the ship. His cabin was small, but it was his own, and for that he was thankful. Growing up, he'd shared his room with five of his siblings.

Where would he be if he'd simply accepted his parents' life as his own?

He looked at the stash of books he'd brought with him to read on his trip around the world. He'd wondered at the time if he'd be able to get through them all, but now, less than halfway through the trip, he was more worried that he'd run out of material. Though he liked Mario and Anna and the other crew members, he hadn't formed any real friends on the *Palanquin*. Off-duty hours were generally spent in the crew lounge, bitching about the passengers, an activity that had bored Adam within the week. He'd taken to spending most of his downtime alone in his cabin, reading more philosophy texts and writing in his journal. He'd signed on to the *Palanquin* to see the world, but he might have done better getting a job at the docks back in Annapolis and spending his spare time at the library.

He dug through his stack of books until he found one on marine biology, curious to learn more about the reef fish poison Mario had mentioned. When the crew had seen him load his boxes of books on board, they'd joked he'd capsize them with the weight of his collection. He'd seen a few of his fellow crew members with the occasional novel, and the engineers liked to read sailing magazines and other technical papers, but no one understood why the paltry crew lounge library would never be enough to satisfy him.

Adam had spent eighteen years of his life with one book. Now he'd never stop until he'd read them all.

three

"COME ON, BABY, DON'T BE SO DIFFICULT."

Kalina shook her head as her stomach solidified into lead. "No. You know this, Bran. You know this. I don't do helicopters."

"Pierre's a great pilot—"

"I don't do helicopters!" she shrieked. Jesus, why wouldn't he listen?

Bran held his hands up in surrender. "Fine. Then you aren't going to port. I'm not getting out the boat and finding some scab to break the taxi strike just for you."

"Fine!" She flopped back on the bed as the door slammed. She flung a hand over her eyes as they started to burn. She needed eye drops. This sea air always made them so dry. But eye drops required moving, and she didn't want to move.

Even before the crash, Kalina had hated helicopters. So loud, so open. When her parents used to take her in theirs to avoid Manhattan traffic, she'd shied away from the floor to ceiling windows. Nothing shaped this way had any business being airborne. She'd felt like a dragonfly about to be swatted from the sky. In her nightmares, she sometimes saw it, a shiny black bug tumbling down, down, down. Splat.

Not that she had any idea what the crash site actually looked like. Her grandfather had hidden the newspapers for a straight week.

Kalina stayed in bed until the sound of helicopter blades faded into the distance. Her jaw unclenched, and she worked up the effort to roll into a sitting position, tugging her black silk negligee down over her thighs. With any luck, Bran would be gone the rest of the day. She couldn't deal with him right now. Couldn't deal with anyone.

Her head was pounding again, so she popped a few aspirin and chased them with a shot of vodka. They were out of the good stuff until the others came back from their trip to port.

She glanced out the window at the bright, cloudless sky. The deck was too much for her today. She turned back inside. Although, if she was alone on the boat...

Quickly, she hurried to her cabinet and rooted around through her lingerie drawer until her fingers closed around a rectangular shape. No one would see her or laugh. Opening up the gleaming wood and brass cabinets to reveal the cabin TV, she slid the tape into the VHS player.

As the lion roared and the familiar title card flashed across the screen, Kalina smiled and snuggled into the covers.

This movie was her guilty pleasure. She'd wandered into a movie theater one rainy afternoon last year and seen a poster of two lovers poised to kiss against a fairy tale backdrop. Everything else at the theater was guns and car chases, so a film about princesses and brides stood out. She'd bought a ticket and some gummy bears and settled in for some mindless entertainment.

What she found was a whole new world of pirates and princesses, giants and swordsmen, humor and heart. There was poison and torture and daring escapes, and all in the name of true love between a princess and a simple farm boy. But her favorite part—the part that brought Kalina back to the theater over half a dozen times in the weeks that followed, was that the whole thing was a story, a beautiful fairy tale invented by a grandfather to tell a sick little boy. Whenever the tale turned scary, it would stop and you'd see the old man reassuring his sick grandson that it was just a story and the princess wouldn't get eaten by shrieking eels and true love would conquer all and that everything would come out all right in the end.

Kalina's grandfather had been like that, once. After her parents' death, he'd moved her out of their apartment and into his house on Long Island. He'd instituted family dinner nights and made sure they talked about their days —what he did at work, what she did at school. He wasn't going to replace her parents and he didn't try to. But he was there for her. At least until she turned fourteen.

For the past six years he was hardly anywhere.

After the movie vanished from the theaters, Kalina found out it was based on a book, so she bought that too, though the story in the book turned out to be somewhat different. The princess part was pretty much the same, but instead of a grandfather and a sick kid, the book's narrator was cynical and grown and didn't like his son and said the whole book was based on a story his father had once told him from "the old country."

Which was cool and all, but Kalina liked the movie version better. She was so relieved earlier this year when she'd found a VHS tape in a video store, though lately she'd been considering buying a spare copy. She'd almost worn through this one with countless rewatchings.

Then again, she basically had the whole film memorized by now. Ooh, this part. This was her favorite part. Where the princess and the black-clad pirate stop to rest on the hillside, and he teases her savagely about him killing the boy she once loved.

"Poor and perfect," Kalina mouthed alongside the princess, "with eyes like the sea after a storm."

A chill rushed over her skin. She must have heard that line dozens of times and never thought anything of it. It was just a pretty, poetic thing for a princess to say about her true love. But she'd seen eyes like that, hadn't she?

Adam, the deckhand. When she'd looked into his eyes the other day, she'd seen a storm for sure. Only Adam's storm hadn't passed. It was yet to come.

Kalina buried herself more deeply under the covers as the princess and pirate shouted hateful things at each other. Ever since she'd hit puberty, men loved to look at her. They looked on her with lust and greed and pleasure. They looked on her with hope and awe and annoyance. But it had been years since anyone ever looked at her like Adam had.

Like he was disappointed.

Now the hero was tumbling down the side of a ravine, shouting out his catch phrase: *As you wish*, which was the secret way he used to tell the princess that he loved her. Kalina's heart soared.

Later, the lovers were reunited at the base of the cliff, and maybe the little boy on the screen didn't like the kissing parts of this movie, but Kalina sure did. She loved the way the hero kissed his princess, like a kiss was all he'd ever wanted. Not like Kalina's lovers, where a kiss was something to get out of the way, an uncomfortable but necessary prelude to the real action.

A shrill, whiny drilling sound invaded the cabin, ruining Buttercup and Westley's tender moment. Kalina sat up in bed. The sound cut off.

But as soon as the lovers reached the Fire Swamp, it started back up again. *Whirrrrz. Whirrrrriiizzzzzzz. Whirzzz. Whirzzz.* What the hell? Kalina threw the covers off and stood. The drill sound continued, getting louder and more insistent. It seemed to be coming from one of the exterior walls of the cabin. She grabbed her short silk robe and threw it over her slip, then opened the door on that side, the one leading out to the deck.

Adam the deckhand was standing just outside her door with a toolbox at his feet, a power drill in his hand and safety goggles pulled down over his stormy eyes.

"What the hell are you doing?" she cried out over the buzz.

Adam turned his head and the drill stopped, leaving behind an uneasy silence. Slowly, he pulled the goggles down until they hung around his neck and looked at her. Kalina had been right about his eyes. Stormclouds gathered in their depths, like a farm boy and a pirate all tangled up in one.

His gaze traveled from the tips of her pink-painted toes, up her legs to the too-short hem of her nightgown grazing the tops of her thighs, and farther up, to her neckline, where she could feel her nipples suddenly hardening against the silk bodice, and finally, up to her face. His expression never changed a bit, but Kalina felt like he'd stripped her bare.

"The power plate over your door was cracked. I'm just installing a new one." He gestured to the work order at his feet. He wasn't even wearing his regulation uniform, just a t-shirt and his khaki pants.

Kalina tugged the sides of her robe shut. "I'm sure you know you're not supposed to do loud or invasive work while the passengers are sleeping."

"I'm sorry, miss," he said. "I thought everyone had gone to shore."

"Well, you can see I haven't."

"Yes, miss."

"So cut it out."

"Yes, miss."

Ugh. What was his problem? "Stop saying that."

Adam lowered the drill. "What?"

"'Yes, miss.' You sound…" What? He sounded perfectly fine. There was nothing in his words or tone that was the slightest bit disrespectful. No one would think so. No one but Kalina, who saw the storm brewing behind his eyes. "Just stop saying it, okay? You sound like a moron."

Adam stood there before her in complete silence.

She blinked at him. "What's your damage?"

He smirked, raising his eyebrows, then nodded and gestured to her like he was acting out a round of charades. *Yes. Miss.*

She groaned through her teeth. "You know what I mean. Turn off the drill, get off my deck, leave me alone. And don't you dare say 'yes, miss' again."

All traces of amusement vanished from his face. He bent to place the drill back into the box and spread his arms in an exaggerated mockery of a sweeping bow.

"As you wish."

As you wish. Kalina froze. How did he know that line? "What did you just say?"

Adam wiped at his brow with the back of his hand. "Huh?"

"Have you been *spying* on me?"

To paraphrase Princess Buttercup, this deckhand had mocked her for the very last time.

four

ADAM STARED AT THE GIRL, utterly baffled. "Pardon me?"

She hadn't liked it when he'd said *yes, miss,* which is what his supervisor had instructed. He didn't think she'd care for *ma'am*, either. So what was he supposed to say to indicate he was following her orders?

"You pervert! You've been watching me!"

"What?" He dropped any pretense at subservience this time. Spying on her? He didn't even know she was in the cabin. Besides, what kind of creep announced his presence with a power drill? "I have no idea what you're talking about. I just came to fix the power plate."

"Get out of my sight!" she yelled at him. "If I ever catch you sneaking around again, you're fired."

Adam could hardly believe the words coming out of her mouth. He'd spent weeks judiciously avoiding any contact with the passengers for just this reason. They were all crazy. He hadn't done a thing.

"You're… wrong!" he blurted. "You're just… wrong."

She flinched as if he'd raised a hand at her. As if being wrong at anything was utterly inconceivable for an empress such as herself. But just as quickly, she recovered, standing up straight and somehow managing to look down at him, even though she was a good eight inches shorter. Her eyes blazed, her hair floated in the breeze. Adam wouldn't have been surprised to see a lightning bolt materialize in her hand as if she were some kind of avenging goddess.

"Well, *you're* fired. As soon as my boyfriend gets back, I'll see to it that you never work on a boat again. What do you think of that?" She crossed her arms over her chest, as if daring him to respond.

But Adam had taken on people far scarier than a coked-up heiress.

"Fine." Adam whipped the safety goggles off his head and threw them—hard—into the toolbox. "I've had enough of this crap, anyway. This is the worst job I've ever had." He leaned forward and dropped his voice to a low growl. "And I've dug irrigation ditches in a desert in New Mexico."

She narrowed her eyes in disdain. "Yeah, right," she scoffed. "This job is so awful. Luxury yacht, see the world, hot chicks coming on to you day and night…"

"Oh, is that what you call you and your friends' little games?" The gloves were off now. If he was fired, he didn't care what he said. "Was it a game when your boyfriend left Anna at the last port? Please, Miss St. Claire, tell us poor underlings the rules so we can at least have a fighting chance. The way I see it, we're screwed if we don't play, but *doubly* screwed if we do."

She stared at him for several seconds, breathing hard, her nostrils actually flaring. But she didn't say anything, and as the unnatural quiet spread between them, Adam felt the urge to reach out and snatch those words back.

"You just made the biggest mistake of your life," she whispered at last, then stomped back into her cabin and slammed the door so hard the new power plate slid off the wall and cracked into pieces on the deck.

Adam frowned and looked down at the mess. Guess it was someone else's problem now. He kicked the open toolbox with his toe and started down the walk toward the staff quarters. But halfway there, he stopped, clenching his hands into fists at his sides.

Leaving the toolbox there was not going to hurt Kalina one bit. She was shut away in her cabin, and the other passengers were off at port. But some other deckhand was going to have to clean up Adam's mess, and as much as he didn't want to lift a finger on behalf of the soulless jerks in charge of this boat, he knew his coworkers deserved better. After all, they were the ones stuck here. Now, at least, Adam could go home and wash off the stench of too much money and too little sense.

Everything he'd said to Kalina had been the truth. Even the bit about the ditch digging. He'd done it at thirteen, when his father expanded the pasture, and the work had made his backache and the skin on his neck and shoulders boil in the hot desert sun. But every night he would gingerly climb into the bed he shared with two of his brothers, secure in the knowledge that the work he'd done was good and necessary and helped provide for his family and the animals of the farm.

What did he do here? Fetch cocktails and gas up jet skis for spoiled brats? Good riddance.

Back at the stateroom door, Adam bent to pick up the tools and put them all away. Maybe he'd grown soft in these years at St. John's. He wondered if there was any truth to Kalina's remarks. Perhaps, if he were transported to New Mexico again, he'd long for a job that brought with it sea breezes and one's own cabin.

It was true though. This job would have been perfect, were it not for his terrible employers. He closed up the toolbox and started to stand, when he heard voices within the stateroom.

Great, she was calling Bran Nesbit already. Adam pressed his head against the wall to see if he could make out any of the lies she was probably telling, but instead of Kalina's voice, she heard another woman's. And strange, metallic clanging.

Odd. He peeked over the windowsill. Oh, that explained it. The TV was blaring, showing some kind of old-fashioned show with kings and queens.

Adam didn't really get TV. Naturally, there was no television at the ranch, and he didn't understand the fascination his friends at school seemed to have with sitcoms. Who wanted to sit around looking at ads for toothpaste and hair regrowth formula for ten minutes just to watch an inane, twenty-minute farce? Books lasted longer, and never had commercials interrupting the fun.

Adam angled his head to see Kalina watching the screen, rapt, as two characters got into a swordfight.

Well, at least that seemed like interesting television. And then it broke for a commercial—probably cold medicine, seeing as there was a grandfatherly sort sitting at a child's bedside. And yet Kalina still stared at the screen, mouthing words along with the characters in the commercial as if it were Shakespearean drama.

She must be really high today. How else to explain her bizarre accusations? Then again, Adam actually *was* spying on her this time. He grabbed the toolbox handle and left the vicinity before she caught him. Not that it would make much of a difference — he was fired either way, right?

Adam breathed in deeply, then let it out, long and slow. The day he left his parent's ranch, he'd sworn to himself that he'd never allow himself to become trapped. The only person who got to choose the type of life he'd lead was Adam—where he'd go and what he'd do for work. If Adam refused the overbearing behavior of his parents, who had raised him and who he still loved, despite everything, there was no way he'd take abuse from a bunch of spoiled rich kids, who held over him nothing more than a paycheck. There was a whole wide world out there, places that not even the imperious Kalina St. Claire could control.

The tension left his shoulders, and Adam smiled. He was practically whistling by the time he got back to the crew lounge.

"*Hola, amigo*," said Mario, looking up from a magazine. "*Qué pasa?*"

"Best day ever," Adam replied. He grabbed a soda from the fridge. "I just got fired."

Mario put down his beer. "What?"

"Sacked," Adam said, and sat down across from his friend with a satisfied sigh. "They'll probably kick me off at the next port. Or, you know, just pitch me over the side. Either way, I'm out of here. And I couldn't be happier."

"You talk to the other deckhands?" Mario asked. "I bet *they* could be happier. We're bleeding staff pretty heavy these days."

"Sorry, man," Adam said. "I hate to leave you all in the lurch, but I can't take the crazy any longer."

"What did you do?"

"Tried to fix a power plate over the master cabin without realizing that Princess Snow was still sleeping off a bender inside."

"Oh," said Mario, with an odd little frown. "Yeah. Miss St. Claire is still on board. She doesn't do helicopters."

"Must have missed that in their endless preference sheets." He took a swig of his soda.

"Her parents died in a crash."

Adam nearly choked. "That's terrible," he blurted out. And it would certainly explain her raw nerves, perhaps more charitably than the usual post-party hangover.

"But she fired you over it?"

Adam sighed. "I don't know what she fired me over, actually. I didn't realize she was there and she started yelling at me, and I tried to apologize, but she was being such a bitch…"

"Ah." Mario nodded. "You opened your mouth."

"Yeah." Adam shrugged and lifted his soda in salute. "*Adiós.*"

Mario shook out his newspaper. "Don't worry about it. She'll cool down."

Right, for at least as long as her next high lasted. "I don't know if I want her to. I don't think I'm cut out for this job."

"What do you mean? There's nothing to it."

"I don't like serving these people."

Mario snorted. "College boy. You don't like serving these people because you want to be one of them."

"Never," Adam replied, glaring.

"No," Mario replied. "I mean, you think you are better than they are."

"I think pretty much everyone is better than they are, Mario. I'd be your deckhand in a heartbeat."

"When I have a yacht, I'll hold you to it." Mario looked at him thoughtfully. "You know, you want that girl to cool down fast, you might think of heating her up." He waggled his eyebrows suggestively. "Boyfriend's gone to shore. Maybe she's lonely."

Adam recoiled. "Gross, man."

"What? She's pretty!"

Sure, Kalina had been pretty—more than pretty—in her silk nightgown with her hair all wild. "My job description is deck and sailing maintenance. Not prostitution."

"You funny or something?" Mario scoffed.

"No. But I'm not playing that game." Adam had some standards — maybe not the kind his parents wanted for him, but some. "Besides, that kind of thing didn't help Anna."

Mario threw up his hands in surrender. "See? You think you're too good for them. Most men in your position would be happy for the extra tips. I know I would. I see the way the girls look at you. They'd eat you up, amigo."

"Yeah," said Adam, "They would. And spit me out afterward."

The light board mounted in the break room began to flash. A call was coming in from the master stateroom.

Mario turned on the intercom. "Yes, Miss St. Claire?"

"Can you send me some breakfast? A nutritional shake?"

Mario made a face. "Of course, miss." He shook his head as he let go of the button. "More garbage. All they ever eat is trash."

He went down to the galley then returned with a silver tray, on which sat a nutritional shake in a stemmed crystal glass, garnished with a strawberry and an orchid. He held the tray out to Adam.

"Go deliver this and make nice with her."

Adam folded his arms. "No way. I'm fine being fired."

"You say that now, but you're not going to have any money at the end of the summer. Go deliver this terrible excuse for a frappe to our bitch of a boss and make her smile." He grinned wolfishly at Adam.

"Definitely not doing that," Adam said, snatching the tray. "But I'll deliver it. And… apologize."

Mario looked skeptical. "My idea's better. But you do what you want."

Adam put the tray on the table, rushed down to his cabin and quickly changed into his uniform. The advice he was willing to take from Mario was that if he was going to do something, he'd do it right.

Looking presentable again, Adam picked up the tray and headed up to the cabin. He steeled his nerves outside the stateroom and knocked.

"Come in."

Okay. Adam took a deep breath. He'd confronted scarier people than Kalina St. Claire. Like his father.

The room was dim, as it had been before, and the TV screen glowed a fuzzy blue. Adam kept his eyes averted from the figure on the bed. "Where may I put this?" he asked in his most respectful voice.

There was no answer. He looked over to catch the tail end of Kalina's shocked expression, as she was already schooling her features into a superior smile.

"Have you come to grovel?" She sat up on the cushions.

"No, miss" he replied, in as even a tone as he could manage. "I've come to bring you breakfast." He gestured to the tray again. "Would you like it in bed?"

The second the words escaped his lips, Adam's mouth clamped shut, as his cheeks and neck heated. That's not how he'd meant it, but somehow, the sentence sounded suggestive.

A single, sculpted eyebrow lifted on her face and her lips pursed smugly. Because this was what she was expecting, wasn't it? For him to come and beg for his job back in the way Mario had recommended.

Adam averted his eyes from her long, tan legs shifting under the short hem of her negligee.

"I mean, the tray. Do you want the tray—"

"In bed?" Kalina finished coyly.

"Yes," Adam ground out.

She sighed, as if contemplating options over where her servant might place her breakfast tray was entirely too taxing for almost noon. "Fine."

Keeping his gaze trained on the shake, he pulled down the tray stands, bent, and set the tray lightly across her lap. "There you are."

"Thank you." The response was automatic. She always said thank you—one of the few who bothered. But it didn't mean anything. It was a reflex, not actual gratitude.

And yet, his eyes lifted to hers again. She stared back, as if searching his face for... something. The smug, satisfied look was gone, and for a second, Adam imagined he could see the girl who wouldn't ride helicopters because her parents had died in a crash. She looked almost human, or as close to human as any of these people could get.

"Miss St. Claire," he began, "I'm... sorry for snapping at you earlier. It was very rude of me."

"Thank you," she repeated. "I'm..." she hesitated, then turned her face away. "I'm very tired. If you could please leave me alone now."

Adam straightened abruptly. For a moment, he'd thought she might apologize, too. How silly of him. People like Kalina St. Claire would never lower themselves like that before a servant. He headed toward the door, but as soon as his hand touched the handle, she spoke again.

"Adam?"

The sound of his name on her lips stopped him dead. He hadn't been sure she even knew it. She'd certainly never used it before. "Yes?"

"I... I won't tell Bran."

Adam left the room without another word.

five

FAR ABOVE THE MASTS OF THE *PALANQUIN*, stars twinkled in the midnight sky, but no one on board seemed to notice or care. From far away, the yacht would appear an island of lights and pulsing music, deep in the heart of a black and silent sea.

On the deck, the party was in full swing. Vodka and pills, champagne and snow, they were stocked and ready to rock. Someone had gotten sick on the upper patio, and Mirelle had poured a bottle of champagne over the vomit to try to wash it away, though all that had succeeded in doing was smearing the mess all over the deck. It stank, so they'd all moved into the lounge and called the staff to clean up. In the lounge, Tim had set the stereo to earsplitting levels and was blasting out Poison and George Michael while the ladies danced on the sofas.

By the time they hit Guns n' Roses, the boys had joined them on the sofas, and were making a game of yanking on the ties of their bikini tops. Mirelle had just shrugged hers off and was dancing topless, while Stevie and Decker were fooling around as she slapped his hands away from hers.

Kalina rolled her eyes. Those two were fucking for two reasons only: they were the only unmatched set on board and Stevie had never managed to get Adam to take her up on her multiple offers. She hoped Stevie was making clear to Decker that they were finished once she got back home and could get with a real man. Decker was a loser. Anyone could see that. God, it must sting to come in second choice to the help.

She missed a beat of the music, and nearly toppled off the couch. Righting herself, Kalina shook her head. That's what came of wasting brain cells on thoughts of Adam. He was lucky he still had a job. It was stupid, what she'd said to him in her cabin the other day. Stupid and impulsive. He gives one half-hearted apology and looks at her with those storm-swept eyes and she lets him walk all over her?

One of these days, her grandfather would die, and she'd be running his company, with thousands of people under her employ, and she couldn't even fire a deckhand who'd spied on her and then abused her to her face.

She hopped off the couch. Another drink. Definitely another drink. She wasn't nearly gone enough if she had mental space for that idiot.

Kalina still didn't know what to make of that moment in her bedroom. Last thing she knew, they'd been screaming at each other and she'd fired him. And then he showed up, dressed in his service outfit, and...

And what? Served her breakfast. Technically. Everything Adam did had an asterisk attached to it, like he was an actor playing the part of a waiter, a deckhand, a servant. When he looked at her, Kalina felt naked. Knowing he'd caught her watching some silly movie was a hundred times worse than even the ridicule she might catch from Bran.

But there'd been no teasing in his eyes in her cabin. When he'd apologized, he'd meant it. Some strange kind of sorrow was written all over his features as he'd leaned over her in bed and held her gaze. For a second, she thought there might have been something else coming, but of course not. He'd practically tripped all over himself just to say the word *bed*.

Stevie told her earlier that she thought he was gay, which would explain a lot. But the homos she'd met hadn't had a problem flirting with women, and Adam didn't even flirt. So maybe he had meant what he'd said during their fight. He didn't take Stevie up on her offers because he thought they were all gross.

The music pounded. Kalina put her hand to her head. She needed more than a drink now. Another bump, maybe, to finish out the party in style. Adjusting her string bikini top, she slipped into her stateroom to grab some coke.

The bathroom light flickered as she retrieved a vial from her cosmetics bag and tapped out a line onto a hand mirror. She bent to snort the line and as she straightened, she caught sight of Bran behind her.

"There you are, baby," he slurred, slipping his arm around her waist. "Hiding away?"

The cocaine buzzed through her system, setting her nerve endings on fire. "Taking a break. Want to dance?"

"No." He grinned at her and pumped his hips in her direction. "I want you."

When he kissed her, he tasted like cigars and gin, and he swirled his tongue inside her mouth as if he had to paint every inch with the scent. Kalina swallowed back her urge to gag and kissed him back, draping her arms over his shoulders and through the longer hair at his neck.

He whirled her out of the bathroom before she could make sure she'd gotten every grain of the coke. "Bran!" she said, pulling away. "Watch it!"

"I'm a caveman, baby." He shoved her backwards onto the bed and pounded his chest with his fists. "I need my woman *now*."

Kalina smiled as he jumped on top of her and yanked her shorts and bikini bottoms down her thighs. Def Leppard's "Pour Some Sugar on Me" thumped through from the other room as he tore off the string top and slingshotted it behind the bed. He licked his lips and looked down on her like he'd uncovered some kind of primal feast.

"Wow, you're ready to go, aren't you?" She slipped her hand inside his board shorts to find him still soft. "Bran, honey?"

He grabbed her by the wrist and yanked her arm away, pinning it with her other hand above her head. He kicked his shorts off and slammed down on her, kneeing her legs open. "Oh, yeah, baby," he grunted in her ear. "Spread your legs for me."

Kalina did as she was told and Bran stuck a finger inside her, pumping back and forth a few times. He kissed her again, grinding his jaw against hers hard. She could feel his free hand between her thighs, and then it was gone, though she could tell by the movement of his shoulders he was tugging on himself, trying to get hard enough to get inside her.

She swallowed. This was always the problem when he got too drunk. After a second, he let go of her wrists and propped himself up with that hand, jerking the other up and down his half-erection.

Kalina arched her back. "Come on, baby," she moaned, in a pretty good imitation of a woman on fire with lust. "I need you so bad."

There. Either that or his hand did it. He was inside her, humping away. Hard. Wow, she'd be sore tomorrow. The drinks and the coke dulled the edges of the pain tonight though.

"You like that?" he was groaning over her now. His face glistened with perspiration, and in the soft recessed lighting over the bed, his skin was a deep pink, like a cartoon pig.

"Yes," she whispered. She slid her arms around his back, pulling her thighs up.

He grabbed her hands and pinned them above her head again, pressing them down into the mattress so his elbows dug into the soft flesh of her forearms.

"Oww. Bran!" She tried to shift but he only squeezed her wrists tighter.

"Yeah. That's right. Take it all," he grunted, thrusting harder.

Kalina winced. There'd definitely be some soreness tomorrow. She didn't mind a little bit of rough play, but Bran never knew when to stop. She wiggled free from his grip and tried to put her arms back around him.

He tried to thrust into her again, but started going soft. "Shit." He reached down and began fisting his dick again. "Hold still."

Def Leppard gave way to Michael Jackson and the electric beats of "Dirty Diana."

She dropped her head back to the mattress. This was going to suck. He'd be working on and off on top of her for the next half hour, at least. She was going to spend her whole, luscious high writhing on the bed, hoping to get him off so she could return to the party.

"Hey, Bran?" she asked, as he tugged himself. "Want to go back outside?"

"No, I've got it." But he clearly didn't. His penis dangled out of the ends of his hands, despite his insistent jerking. Outside, Michael Jackson wailed about all the dirty things Diana would do to him. Kalina wondered if Diana ever just closed her eyes and waited for it to end.

Bran crawled up her body, knees on either side of her chest, and slapped his dick against her face. "Suck me, baby."

Kalina sealed her lips and turned her face away. His soft dick flopped on her ear and stuck to strands of her hair.

He grabbed her by the chin and turned her face back towards his limp penis. "Come on, Kiki. Suck me. Make it nice and hard."

Diana might be a freak the boys could taunt, but Kalina St. Claire was anything but.

She batted his penis away and scooted into a sitting position. "No, Bran, quit it."

"What's wrong?"

She rolled her eyes and glared at him. "Are you kidding? Not when your cock still tastes like that whore."

Kalina never even saw it coming. One second she was mouthing off to Bran and the next second she was face down on the mattress, her cheek burning like it had been lit on fire. She clapped a hand to her face and struggled to breathe.

"Dammit, Kalina." Bran was shaking out his hand. "What the hell?"

What the hell? *What the hell?* Kalina had never been slapped in her life. She blinked at Bran, dumbfounded. Her tongue seemed to have been slapped loose from her mouth.

The rage on Bran's face drooped into recognition, and then fear. "Shit. Kiki…"

He reached for her, but she scrambled off the bed, still holding her throbbing cheek. Her jaw ached, and her left eye watered uncontrollably. Half-blind, she rooted around in the nearest cabinet for clothing. Any clothing. An old nightshirt. Fine. She swiped her cutoffs and bikini bottoms off the floor and practically jumped into them.

Bran circled the end of the bed. "Kiki, let's talk about this."

"Get out of here," she whispered.

He straightened, and his expression turned indignant. "*You* get out of here," he shot back. "This is *my* yacht."

Kalina breathed in. She breathed out. "Fine!" she shouted, whirled and made for the door.

"Wait!" Bran grabbed for her hand, but she shook him off, and rushed back out into the throng of the party. There. Safe.

He would *never* touch her again.

Through blurred eyes, Kalina looked around the room. She didn't see Lisa or Tim, and Stevie had her tongue down Decker's throat. Mirelle and Jorge were still dancing on the sofas, and hardly looked over when she grabbed a bottle of vodka and made for the door.

"What's her problem?" she heard Decker ask as she crossed the threshold onto the deck.

"Must be on the rag," Stevie replied.

Kalina stumbled past the patio and across the upper and lower decks, all the way down the stairs to the stern. There she stood, looking out over the water, as hot tears flowed over her stinging skin.

How far until the next port? How long until she never had to see him again? Cheating with his maid — that was annoying, but acceptable. This… this was not.

Her skin crawled and she shivered, despite the warmth of the tropical night air. She was supposed to have been safe with Bran. He was supposed to love her for *her*, because he had as much money as she did. But he couldn't have loved her at all. This wasn't love, true or otherwise.

She rubbed her sore cheek and listened to the water lapping against the side of the boat. No one was coming for her. Maybe they were all back with Bran, listening to his side of the story while they drank his booze and soaked up his hospitality.

She couldn't stand being on the same boat as that bastard for another minute. She looked over at the nearest lifeboat, rigged up against the side, tucked the vodka into the crook of her arm, and threw her leg over the rail. She was glad no one was around to see her flailing her way into the boat as she tumbled over the side and up against the inflatable bumper.

She tucked herself into the darkest corner and lay her head against the inner cushion as she unscrewed the vodka. This was going to be a long night, and Kalina would need every drop of oblivion this bottle could offer to get through it.

six

THE DOWNSIDE OF NOT BEING FIRED was that Adam's job now entailed cleaning up nearly a gallon's worth of vomit and spilled champagne off the lido deck at two o'clock in the morning.

He never should have apologized to Kalina.

Fifty-four days left, and every single one of them loomed before him, as endless as the Pacific Ocean itself. He finished swabbing the mess, then dry mopped until everything was smooth and shiny again.

Once, out of curiosity, he'd looked up the price sheet for Bran Nesbit's preferred brand of bubbly. Three hundred and forty dollars a bottle. And they used it like Pine-Sol.

Disgusting.

After thoroughly disinfecting the mop, Adam headed back to the janitor's locker to deposit his cleaning supplies. At least the party seemed to have died down. The main cabin was no doubt a complete disaster, but that would be the steward staff's job at five a.m. The deck was done for the night.

He ducked into the closet and started to put away the supplies, noting as he did that one of the cabinet doors must have a faulty latch. It hung open and a row of bottles had rolled out, cluttering the floor.

He was off duty. He should really let some other sucker handle it in the morning.

Or maybe the bottles would start leaking tonight and cause a massive cloud of noxious gas to overwhelm the ship.

Sometimes Adam hated his brain. It had been four years since he'd gone with his father on evening rounds, four years since he couldn't shut his eyes until every last shelf was stocked, every last door was checked, every last gun was cleaned, checked and loaded. Until they knew with absolute certainty that if the Apocalypse came that night, they'd be prepared.

If the Apocalypse came for Adam this evening, he'd be dining on caviar and bon bons while he waited for the Devil to scoop up his bosses. Though, according to his parents, he'd be headed to Hell, too. When he'd turned his back on the ranch, it was as good as throwing all they'd taught him back in their faces.

If only they could see him now, fixing a cabinet door in a janitor's closet at two-thirty in the morning. If only they knew about the go-bag he still kept stashed under his bed. He hadn't lost the ranch entirely.

Just traded it for a different set of ills.

By the time he'd finished with the door, Adam could hardly keep his eyes open. He trudged back down into crew quarters, hardly surprised that no one else was up. This was the dead hour, with just a skeleton engineering and navigational crew up, and even too early for the galley staff and stewards to start their days. He headed down the hall, surprised to see two doors ajar. Great, more bad locks to fix tomorrow. He pulled them each shut and went for his own cabin.

As soon as he touched the handle, a chill shot down his spine. Also ajar. He pushed the door open and stared into the darkness.

"Anyone in there?" he asked quietly, and flicked on the light.

His pillow had gone from the bed to the floor, but no other change seemed to have happened. Still, unease hung heavy in the cabin, making the narrow, sloping walls seem even tighter.

There was a loud, sharp sound, like a heavy door being slammed. Repeatedly.

Every muscle in Adam's body tensed up. He knew that sound from endless hours of target practice. Gunshots. Some kind of automatic rifle. His father wanted him ready to defend the homestead from invasion during the Tribulation. Adam had learned well.

Maybe the Apocalypse wasn't happening tonight, but something else was, and it was very, very bad.

Out of instinct more than anything, he pulled his go-bag out from under his bed and grabbed a dark, hooded jacket, pulling it on before slipping the bags straps over his shoulders and heading back down the hall. He checked in a few of the other rooms. Empty. All empty.

This was worse than he'd thought. The ship was in trouble.

The radio in the crew lounge was a mass of wires. How had he not seen it when he'd been heading to bed? Carefully, he worked his way up to the navigation deck, where he spotted the first intruder.

Not that there was much to see in the dark. A man, in dark clothes, with a gun that seemed to suck all the air out of Adam's lungs. They'd been boarded.

He ducked behind a lounge chair as another pirate turned onto the walk and started coming his way. Adam crouched in the shadows, his head turned down, not even daring to breathe as the footsteps neared, passed, and vanished down the corridor the way he'd come. After a minute, the other pirate followed.

Adam began to breathe again. In and out. In and out. They'd gone over procedures, of course, for boarding by hostile persons, but they always involved contacting security and radioing for help. If those methods were going to work, wouldn't they already have been tried?

He needed to see if everyone else was okay. As soon as he was certain there were no more pirates coming, he sneaked down the corridor to the galley and peeked in the window.

No. *No*. The words died in Adam's throat. Everything died.

There were bloody handprints on the wall of the galley. Bloody spatters on the gleaming steel countertops. Bodies littering the white-tiled floors. He counted four, five, all the way up to ten — some in their uniforms, some in nightclothes. There was

Beatriz, the stewardess, and Louie the morning deckhand. There was…

There was Mario. Adam stifled a cry in his throat. The cook was splayed face down in a puddle of dark red blood.

Were the pirates murdering everyone on board?

He heard a scream from the upper deck and another gunshot rent the air. Blood rushed in his ears and as he leaned forward to listen up the stairs he saw his hands trembling. He was going to die. They were all going to die.

He should run, now. Get to the back, get in a lifeboat, and take off. It was the only chance. They'd find him eventually.

Mario's body lay cooling on the galley floor, but his words remained in his head. Any job worth doing…

Adam took a deep breath and started tiptoeing up the stairs to the navigation deck.

Halfway up, he could see in the windows of the bridge. All the passengers, a few of the engineers, and the captain stood huddled against one wall, while the pirates sat in the captain's chair and leaned against the burnished controls. The passengers were silent and scared, their eyes red-rimmed. Some appeared worse for wear, with small cuts or abrasions on their arms and faces. Jorge held an arm wrapped in a jacket, seeping blood. The women were crying, and Decker, too. Adam leaned in to do a headcount.

The captain's eyes lifted to the window and met his. The man gave a nearly imperceptible shake of his head.

Adam shrank back into the shadows. Okay, *don't*. Don't what? Don't try to save them? The pirates had already proven willing and eager to murder every low-ranking crew member on board. They'd spared the passengers and the captain. So they were here for ransom. No one who could pay would get shot.

Adam could not count himself among that number.

But what was he supposed to do? Run away? Just…

A shout broke the silence of the night. It was the shout that saved him.

A man stood at the top of the staircase, training his gun on Adam, who took off, half sprinting, half falling down to the main deck. He leapt over the guardrail and down to the lower deck, taking most of the fall on his left knee. Pain exploded outward from his leg, but he'd put another level between him and the men who'd follow. He stood, stumbled once, and kept going, running toward the stern, suddenly glad he knew the layout of this infernal yacht by heart.

Gunshots followed him as he raced, and he knew any second one would find their target. If there were more pirates waiting at the stern, he was dead meat.

There was a body lying on the deck at the stern. Probably the night security. No time to check for the gun. He saw the pirate's boat, tied up to the stern. Was there anyone aboard? Did they see him? He ducked and ran toward the nearest lifeboat.

His memory of the crew safety meeting unspooled in his head at lightning speed. They'd all been instructed on the proper launch of the lifeboats. In the rare, rare, incredibly rare event of needing to use the lifeboats, there was safe speed, speed that was designed not to disturb the passengers, not to make it seem like they were in a life-threatening situation.

Then there was the emergency lever. Adam catapulted into the nearest lifeboat and pulled down the lever. The boat dropped like a stone into the waves.

More gunshots, zipping in the water all around him. He was a veritable sitting duck, bobbing up and down in the empty bathtub of the calm night sea. He turned the key, praying that engineering was keeping to their maintenance schedule. There. *There.* The engine roared to life.

The pirates were still shooting. He needed to get out of here. He turned the boat and sped away from the *Palanquin*, gunning the engine as hard and fast as he dared. Nothing mattered but escaping the pirates. Nothing mattered but getting far enough away that they didn't bother chasing.

The shouts of the pirates vanished behind him, the lights of the *Palanquin* faded into the distance, and after half an hour of hard driving into nothingness, Adam pulled back on the throttle. He let the engine idle, and listened for the sound of speedboats following him, but there was nothing.

He let out a breath. It was possible he hadn't breathed in years. Suddenly boneless, he dropped to his knees on the boat.

In three years, Adam had never spoken a single prayer. He'd turned his back on that life, and he figured that meant he'd turned his back on God as well. But now, in the stillness of that black, black night, he prayed.

He prayed for Beatriz and Louie and the other crew members he'd seen on that bloody galley floor. He prayed for Mario, who had been his friend, and did not deserve to die on the *Palanquin*. He prayed for the passengers and crew members still held hostage, that they would find strength and courage to face their ordeal and come out the other side. And then he prayed for the men who had done this awful thing, that they could find in them the ability to repent and stop harming others.

He also prayed that some fine officer of the law would catch them. Soon.

Then he slumped against the side of the boat, exhausted, empty as a wrung out rag.

"And Lord," he added with a whisper, "Please send someone to find me. I don't want to be out here all alone."

There was a groan, and an unconscious Kalina St. Claire rolled over into his arms.

seven

IT WAS TOO BRIGHT. Had Bran left the shades open again? Stupid luxury stateroom. All those windows meant all that sun. She threw an arm over her eyes and moaned.

And the rocking. It was especially bad today. You'd think they were out to sea in a thimble, the way the boat pitched some nights. Kalina felt her stomach turn over. So it was going to be *that* kind of morning.

She couldn't even get comfortable. It was far too hot, like someone had turned off the air conditioning. Her eyes flickered open and met blue sky instead of cabin ceiling. Kalina bolted into a sitting position, blinking as her eyes adjusted to the light.

And then blinking again, this time in utter disbelief.

She was seated in the bottom of one of the small inflatable lifeboats, with nothing but calm blue sea as far as she could see. And Adam the deckhand was seated across from her.

"Hi," he said. "You're up."

"Where are we?" she croaked. Her tongue stuck to the roof of her mouth. Her stomach flipped again.

Adam turned his head and looked out over the endless water. "The Pacific Ocean."

No shit, Sherlock. But she couldn't even muster annoyance without losing it, as she scrambled to the edge and vomited over the side.

For a second it was nothing but retching noises and the sour flavor of vodka and bile. She coughed and spit into the water, then slumped back down.

Adam was holding out a canteen of water. "Drink," he advised her. "But don't rinse and spit. We've got a limited supply."

Kalina wiped the back of her hand across her face, staring at him in suspicion. Had he kidnapped her? Was this some sort of crazy revenge scheme after she'd threatened to get him fired?

"Where's the boat?" she asked.

He gestured with the water again. "Drink some water, then we'll talk. I don't want you vomiting again. You'll attract sharks."

"I'll *what*?" She took the water. It was lukewarm, but still a relief. She wanted more than anything to swish it around her mouth and spit it out, but swallowed, as Adam had suggested. Until they got back to the *Palanquin*, she'd need to keep hydrated at the very least.

How long had they been out here? The sun was high in the sky already. How long had he been sitting here, just watching her sleep?

Adam rooted around in the lifeboat's supply chest. "Beef jerky?"

"What? Eww, no."

He turned to look at her, his brow furrowed in concern. "You should eat something."

"You should tell me what the hell is going on."

Adam abruptly sat down on the floor of the boat. No, he collapsed, as if beneath a heavy weight. He draped his forearms on his raised knees, and let his head hang down. The legs of his pants were grimy, she noted, his right knee caked with dark brownish red streaks like…

Dried blood.

Oh, God, what was going on?

Adam took a deep breath and lifted his head. "There were…" he hesitated, "men on the yacht. In the middle of the night."

Kalina stared at him. "No."

"They took the passengers hostage," he went on, still facing away. "They… they killed most of the crew."

Her stomach started churning again. Her brain clamped down on the word *killed*, refusing to let it roost. He couldn't mean that. He couldn't. "I don't understand. What about my friends?"

"When I found them," he said, "the pirates had all your friends and the bridge crew hostage on the bridge."

"I don't believe it," she whispered, shaking her head. "I don't believe you."

He narrowed his bloodshot eyes at her. "I was there. I saw *my* friends dead on the galley floor."

Kalina looked away. This was impossible. "So why didn't they get us?"

"I don't know."

Kalina turned back to him.

"I was running away. I jumped in the lifeboat and took off. They followed me for a while, but I guess they figured I wasn't going in any useful direction, so they stopped." He shrugged. "I wasn't thinking. I was just running." He gestured to her. "I didn't even know you were in the boat until later."

Her head pounded. Her throat burned. She felt ready to hurl again. And the annoying deckhand claimed he'd just saved her from a bunch of murderous pirates. What could she possibly say?

"I hurt my leg running from them," he said, and yanked up the hem of his pants leg to show her an abrasion on his knee the size of a baseball. "But no, I didn't have time to get a note from the pirates about how they wanted to kill me before I escaped."

She was still quiet, her aching brain trying to process the impossibility of it all. How could she have slept through all of this? Sure, she'd been wasted last night, but not *that* wasted.

"And, honestly," he said as he dropped the hem and folded his arms, "I don't care if you believe me. It doesn't change the situation. We're out here, and we're stuck."

Kalina considered this as she looked at Adam. His stormy eyes were red and glassy, as if he'd had a long, sleepless night. His hair was a mess, his clothing bloody and rumpled. He looked like a man who'd been running for his life. In fact, he looked ready to drop.

Okay. She swallowed, trying not to gag.

"I believe you," she said. "What do we do now?"

"I have no idea." He sounded half-dead. "I'm sorry."

"What?"

"I'm sorry," he repeated. "You'd probably be okay, back on the boat."

"Back on the boat. With the pirates."

"Yes." He looked down. "They weren't shooting you guys. They looked like they were going to hold you for ransom or something."

"I'd be safer being held for ransom at gunpoint?" she asked, blinking. "That's your argument? I thought you were, like, a philosophy major or something."

His eyes widened a fraction as Kalina realized her mistake. Stevie had mentioned it the other day, when she'd asked about Adam.

Stevie, who might be dead now...

"When I drove the boat away," Adam said, "it's because doing that meant I got to stay alive longer than the other crew members did when the pirates caught them. That was the only equation I did. But as survival strategies go, it's not great."

"We're alive," she argued.

"Yeah." He waved vaguely out over the ocean. "But they stopped following us. I can only imagine it's because they realized I wasn't going to get anywhere before I ran out of fuel or died."

She looked at the engine. "Are we? Out of fuel?"

He shook his head. "No. We have about half a tank left."

So Adam had turned off the boat so they wouldn't waste fuel going around in circles. That was a good idea, she supposed.

"Can't we radio for help?"

"The only people I think are likely to be in radio range are the pirates," he said, still not meeting her eyes. "But we can do that. If you want to."

If she wanted to? "You mean we should radio the pirates?"

"Yes." He nodded. "Surrender. They probably won't kill you."

But they would almost certainly kill *him*.

"No," she insisted, appalled. "We aren't going to do that."

Again, he looked surprised. Kalina wanted to punch him in the other knee. Did he really think she was going to order him to return to the boat where people had just murdered the entire crew? Damn. She knew he didn't like her. She hadn't realized he thought she was evil.

"So then we stay out here," he said softly. "And slowly die of exposure and dehydration."

"Don't say that!"

"Have you ever seen something die of exposure, Miss St. Claire? I'm from the desert, remember? It's not pretty."

"And you can stop calling me Miss St. Claire too," she added. "I'm pretty sure any employer-employee distinction goes out the window as soon as you're…"

Trapped on a lifeboat.

"We found this dog once," he continued, as if she'd said nothing. "Me and my brothers. It was trapped in a canyon. We brought it home. Poor thing. Bones and fur, hardly. It wouldn't drink, wouldn't even lift its head."

"Stop," Kalina begged him, her eyes wide.

"My father had to put it down." He closed his eyes. "It's not pretty."

Kalina waited, but he didn't open his eyes again, just sat there, still, his head bowed over his knees.

How long had he been out here, waiting, alone, with nothing but the visions of his dead crewmates to keep him company?

Wait… had he just fallen asleep? She leaned forward to nudge him awake, but stopped. He'd been up all night, he'd seen all his crewmates killed, he'd run for his life — he should get some rest. A little bit of rest so he could actually help her get out of this mess and not just dream up horror stories where they died of dehydration or went back to the ship to get executed by a bunch of bloodthirsty criminals.

Kalina hugged her knees to her chest, chilly despite the warmth of the Pacific sun. She hoped Adam was right, and the men were holding her friends hostage. But even if it were true, how many crew members had been murdered last night?

She wasn't even sure how many people worked on the *Palanquin*. Twenty? Thirty? Somewhere in that neighborhood. Down one, after she'd had Anna fired.

That poor girl. Ironically, her life had been spared by firing her. Unbidden, half-remembered faces of the crew floated up before her. The head steward. The pastry chef. The engineer she always saw in the treadmill at the gym. Were they really all dead?

And… Adam. He'd seen them all. *He* could be dead right now. Insulting her and defying her and staring at her a little too hard one day, and lying on the deck in a pool of his own blood the next.

Kalina couldn't hold it back. She barely raised herself over the side of the boat in time, and all that precious water and bile went spilling into the Pacific. Her eyes watered as she spit into the waves. Damn, she hoped Adam wasn't right about the sharks.

She hoped he wasn't right about a lot of things.

She didn't know how long she sat there, waiting, sipping water and praying for her stomach to stop churning, for her head to stop aching, for her to wake up from this nightmare. As the minutes slid by, she began to understand Adam's perspective. Sitting here was not good. She kept scanning the blue horizon as if looking for a sign of life. She looked around the floor of the boat to see that, at some point, Adam had counted out bottles of water, packages of food and batteries, first aid equipment. Everything was laid in neat little rows. She picked up a flashlight.

"Three days," came a voice behind her. She turned to find him examining her with bloodshot eyes. "We have provisions for three days. Maybe."

"Three days," she said softly, weighing the flashlight in her hands. "If they are ransoming my friends, like you said, they'll want to do it soon, right?"

"Yes."

"Then we'll be able to contact the rescue ships when they come."

Adam considered this for a long moment, and as she watched, his eyes softened, hope lighting up behind the storm clouds. "That might work. We'll check in with the radio from time to time. Maybe we'll hear something promising."

Maybe. Or maybe they'd die out here, like Adam feared.

Oh, crap. She was going to throw up. Again.

eight

LIFEBOATS FOR THE RICH AND FAMOUS should come stocked with a supply of drugs and alcohol on top of the usual survival kits. Because being trapped with a rich girl going through a cocaine hangover made most of their other difficulties seem minor.

He'd never thought he'd say this, but even the sight of her cutoffs-clad bottom bent over the side of the boat was starting to weary him. Especially since it was decidedly less sexy when accompanied by the sound of her tossing her cookies into the surf, yet again.

By the time Adam had given up and dosed Kalina with the anti-nausea seasickness drugs in the medical kit, she'd vomited up nearly an entire bottle of water. Aspirin barely made a dent in her headaches, and as for her mood…

"I can't take this anymore!" she screamed. "There's nothing here. There's nothing on the radio.

There's nothing at all. I can't just sit around and watch the sun move across the sky!"

Adam dug around in his go-bag until he found a pack of cards. He tossed it to her.

"Are you kidding?" Kalina snorted. "We're waiting around to see if we're going to die or not and you want to play poker?"

"Actually," he replied. "I was kind of hoping you'd be in the mood for solitaire."

She screamed and chucked the cards overboard.

Adam considered following it. Something, clearly, had to be done, or they were never going to make it through this. "Have you ever tried meditation?"

She glared at him. "Don't you talk to me about meditation. I've been on retreats in Kyoto."

"Meditation retreats?" he asked.

"Yes."

He nodded, wondering if it was really a meditation retreat, or if that's just what rich folks called a spa vacation with a smattering of Buddhism thrown in. "Okay then, how do you do it?"

"You keep your mouth shut, farm boy." She clapped her hand over her lips and her eyes widened. She got very, very still. Was that what she thought meditation was?

Adam placed his hand over his mouth, copied her cross-legged position and waited. This was not the pose he'd seen in his world religion textbooks.

She lowered her hand and gave him dagger eyes. "What the hell are you doing?"

"Meditating?" he suggested.

She growled at him. Actually growled, like an animal, then turned her back and ignored him for a solid hour.

Adam had never learned how to meditate. His father hadn't held much truck with what he called "that hippie stuff" — but after years of practice at prayer meetings, Adam had gotten very good at sitting still for long periods without getting bored out of his skull. So while Kalina ignored him, he did that. The sound of the waves on the boat was pleasant, and the sun was low enough now that the air had cooled to a comfortable temperature. He wished they could go swimming, but he remembered his training in regards to sharks and splashing. It would probably be better not to draw too much attention to themselves.

There was a running checklist in his head. They had so many liters of water left, so many meals worth of rations. The radio scanner had a solar battery, so he didn't worry about running it down, but so far, they'd heard nothing but static. The white noise and the water combined to make Adam feel sleepy again, especially as the afternoon waned into evening.

After a while, he noticed that Kalina had started moving again. She was running her hands along the inside of the inflated tube keeping the dingy afloat. Adam watched her, curious, as she yanked out what looked like a metal support beam.

"What are you doing?" he asked. "I think that needs to be there."

"Idiot," she sneered, tossing her hair over her shoulder. "You didn't even set this up right." She pulled the support beam out further, revealing a joint, and then, even more amazingly, a tarp. "We have a shelter."

Adam leaned forward to see she was right. There, printed on the underside of the tube, were directions for setting up the boat's emergency shelter. He must not have seen it before because that side of the boat was the one Kalina had been sleeping against.

Kalina found the base for the end of the tent pole and shoved it in, then pulled the tarp down tight around it, forming a small shelter that covered about half of the surface area of the boat. Flaps fell across the opening, with little Velcro fasteners.

"There." She dusted her hands off and looked at her discovery with pride.

"This is great," Adam said. "This will protect us from the elements. Maybe we can even use the tarp to collect water if it rains. And it'll be great to keep the sun off us when it comes up again."

Kalina looked around her. "Yeah, the sun. But there's no sun now, so stay out of my bedroom." Then she scooted inside the tent and flicked the flaps closed.

"Are you kidding me?" he asked at the blank red tent flaps. "What if it rains?"

"Collect water, like you said."

"So we're back to employee and employer again?"

"We're back to you have been acting all high and mighty about our rations or whatever all day, and you didn't even know we had a *tent*." Her voice floated out of the tent, snide and superior.

"That's because you spent half the day passed out against it, and the other half vomiting all over it."

She stuck her head out of the flaps and glared at him. "I did *not* throw up on the boat. I was very careful."

"You have a lot of practice, I'm sure."

Now her whole upper half was out. "What the hell is that supposed to mean?"

Adam gave her a look. "Are you serious? Can you name the last day you didn't wake up hungover?"

Kalina opened her mouth, then shut it again.

"I'm the one trying to help us survive," Adam said. "You're the one throwing a perfectly good deck of playing cards into the ocean. And a good half a liter of water, too."

"It comes out one side or the other, Adam. At least with the tent we can arrange for a little privacy there, too."

His mouth opened, and she smiled smugly, clearly triumphant that she'd managed to shock him by talking about their bodily functions.

He sighed. "Look, I'm sorry I made a mistake. But we found it, before either of us roasted to a crisp."

"That doesn't mean I'm letting you sleep with me."

"I don't want to—" Adam shook his head, trying to clear it of the image of curling up with Kalina under a blanket of southern stars. "Look, I don't think we should sleep at the same time, at all."

"What?" She cocked her head. She made quite a picture there, on her knees at the entrance of the tent, her wind-tossed hair blowing about in the twilight breeze. Pretty soon, it would be too dark to see her at all.

"Someone has to remain awake at all times to listen to the radio. We should sleep in shifts."

"Fine by me," she said. "It means I only have to look at you eight hours of the day." She disappeared back inside the tent. "You slept last, so I'll take the first shift tonight."

He saw one of the flashlights click on, illuminating the shelter with an inviting, rosy glow. Her silhouette shadowed the wall of the tent as she shook out her hair and gathered it up into a big coil on top of her head. She stretched, lifting her arms up above her head and bending backwards. As her nightshirt fell away from her body, its sheerness was highlighted in the silhouette. He could see every curve of her body.

"Don't waste the batteries," he said, though his tone was more snappish than he'd intended.

Her shadow turned in his direction. "Sorry."

The light went off, leaving Adam alone beneath the indigo sky. The water lapped against the sides of the boat. Every time Kalina shifted, the fabric whispered and the boat rocked. It was impossible to forget she was little more than a scrap of tarpaulin away.

He wondered what she was going to do if she had to vomit again. Would she be able to control herself enough to make it out of the shelter? He opened his mouth to ask, but then shut it again. Maybe Kalina was right — it would be best if they kept their conversations to a minimum. They could hardly speak without fighting as it was.

As long as he had the deck to himself, he might as well respond to nature's call. At least he didn't have to ask her to turn around or anything. After that, he took another drink of water, and ate about half of his evening ration, but he had little appetite. Was there any chance at all of this ending well?

They should have heard something on the radio by now, even if it was just the pirates. If there was any rescue attempt to be made, it would be made soon. Or, they could be out of radio range. The Pacific was a really, really big place. Things got lost here all the time. Boats, planes, entire islands. Nothing but specks against the endless blue.

And of all the people to fight for survival with, why did it have to be the most spoiled bitch on the *Palanquin*? Even in an emergency, she couldn't act normal. For a short moment earlier this afternoon, he thought she'd be a human — she had seemed truly disturbed by the news of the crew's deaths, and shocked by his suggestion that they surrender. He'd mistakenly believed that she cared one iota whether he lived or died.

But no. Of course not. He was a deckhand on the *Palanquin*, and he was a deckhand on the lifeboat too. And he made one little mistake as to the layout of the dinghy, and she seemed ready to have him chucked overboard like he was no more than a game she wasn't in the mood for.

At least Adam had his anger to keep him awake. Fear worked for a while, but it was also really draining, whereas the more he recounted the things he hated about Kalina St. Claire, the more revved up he felt.

Her weight shifted again, and the boat tilted slightly as she rolled over.

This was going to be a very long night. What he wouldn't give for a pack of playing cards. Stupid Kalina.

The last of the light faded, and the stars flickered to life in the bowl of the black sky. Adam lay back on the floor of the boat, his head as close to the tent flaps as he dared, and stared up the stars.

Growing up in the desert, Adam had become very familiar with the night sky and the Milky Way, and ever since getting to the South Pacific, he'd made sure to take his star charts out on deck every night and try to orient himself to the new sky. It had been difficult most nights, as Bran and his guests liked to shine every light on the ship and hide the stars, even on nights they were far from port. He'd taken to getting up early and mapping the morning sky.

The sky down here was strange—so familiar, and yet so different. There was his old buddy Orion, the hunter. Adam always spotted him first, like a touch of home on the other side of the world. The orient formation down here was trickier than back home. South was found by first locating the Southern Cross, a tiny constellation half-hidden in Centaurus, then tracing its length four and a half times over. The Big Dipper, and its route to the pole star, was so much easier.

At least his go-bag was equipped with a compass. If they were navigating by stars, they were well and truly screwed.

Time passed in a wash of stars and static, and soft, shushing waves. And then a new sound met his ears, jarring him out of —well, he wasn't asleep. Not really.

For the first few seconds, Adam couldn't place it at all, though he'd swear he knew this sound well. He sat up and it vanished. He lay down again.

Sobbing. Nearly silent, little more than gulping, heaving breaths.

Adam squeezed his eyes shut. Now he could feel it, too, the way her racking cries made the inflated bottom of the boat tremble and shake right beneath his head. She must be just on the other side of the flap.

In total misery.

But what was he supposed to do? Nothing he said could possibly comfort her. They'd heard nothing on the radio, not even from the pirates. For all Adam knew, they'd lined up the passengers and executed them. There was no land nearby. Little chance of a random boat passing close enough to see. They'd probably die out here, together, sniping at each other until they cured like mummies in the salt sea air.

Yeah, he definitely wouldn't say any of those things.

The sobs continued, mute and monstrous, for several minutes. He couldn't take it anymore. He rolled over and looked at the tent. In the light from the moon and stars, he could see the tips of her fingers peeking out from beneath the flap.

He reached out and touched her. Her fingers twined with his and held tight.

That was all. He lay his head back down, gently, as if the movement might disturb her. Her fingertip grip was strong, nearly desperate. That's all it was, of course. Desperation. She'd probably die before she ever touched another person.

He breathed deeply and slowly, as her fear shuddered the deck beneath them and her fingers curled around his in a death grip. He didn't know when she stopped crying. He didn't know when he fell asleep. But he never once let go of her hand.

nine

CRYSTALS OF SALT CRACKLED on her eyelashes as Kalina awoke. They'd been more common in the last few mornings — salt dusting the surface of the boat like sugar on cookies and gathering in corners and hems, making her skin sticky and her clothes itchy and her eyes sting. She lay on the bottom of the boat, staring up at the red ceiling of the tent and trying to unstick her dry tongue from the roof of her dry mouth.

They'd switched shifts after that first night, as they realized Kalina was more accustomed to sleeping late and Adam to rising early. But both were sleeping more and more often. Sleeping distracted from the sheer, utter boredom of the nothingness of the open ocean, from the endless static on the radio, from the rising thirst in their throats. She hadn't been sick anymore, not after that first day, but as their supplies dwindled, she found her thoughts going again and again to the water she'd so carelessly thrown up that first morning.

Even when they weren't sleeping, there wasn't much to talk about. They'd stopped sniping at each other at least. Kalina found it difficult to give him a hard time at all after that first, terrible night, when he'd somehow known exactly what she needed, without her saying it. That wordless, simple comfort of grabbing tight to her hand. He hadn't spoken about it come morning. Hadn't spoken about much at all. It should have felt strange, to be sitting so long in a small boat with another human and saying nothing. Whenever she was at dinner or the back of a limo or at a bar with someone, there was always chatter to be had. But Adam didn't speak. Probably didn't want to make them any thirstier than they already were.

On their second night on the boat, as they'd switched shifts, Adam had given her a long, hard look. "Tomorrow, we signal the pirates," he'd said, as if it wasn't up for discussion. And maybe it was his tone, or the storm clouds gathering in his eyes, but she hadn't even argued.

The next day, they'd done so. No answer. Then they'd gone back to the place where Adam left the *Palanquin*. Nothing. They were alone on the ocean, and nearly out of gas, and they couldn't even arrange to get themselves shot.

She hoped Adam wasn't blaming himself. She was still better off here than in the hands of pirates. There was no telling that any of her friends were alive, or what sorts of horrible things might be happening to them if they were.

Today marked the last dregs in their bottles. After this, they could only pray it would rain. Kalina swallowed, looking up at the tent. She wouldn't cry. Crying wasted water. And it wouldn't do any good anyway.

She should have visited her grandfather more. Sure, he hardly ever so much as remembered her name, but that wasn't his fault. She remembered *him*, so she should have gone, and held his hand or kissed his face or just breathed the same air. Somewhere in there, he loved her, even if he couldn't access that part of his brain anymore.

Kalina wondered who would tell her grandfather she was gone. If they would even hold a funeral. Probably not the SC International board of directors. They'd throw a party and start divvying up her shares of stock.

No wasting water.

She opened up the flap and crawled out of the tent. Adam was sitting near the starboard bow, wearing that ridiculous visor he'd constructed out of an empty cardboard box. He held a knot of fishing line in his hands, dangling it overboard.

He'd been doing that for three days with very little luck.

"Morning," she croaked with her wind-dried voice. It hardly seemed appropriate to add the "good."

"Hi," he said, and gestured to the deck at his side. "Got something."

She looked and saw a few pieces of what must have been a very tiny fish. "Great. What happened to the rest of it?"

He jerked the line. "Bait."

Kalina supposed that made sense. Such a small fish wasn't going to be useful to them for eating.

They might as well see if they could catch anything large with it.

She looked out over the water. She could go blind searching the horizon, and never see anything different. The first day, she'd learned how to tell the difference between a mirage and a boat. It was easy: always mirages. Starboard bow: nothing. Port bow: nothing. Starboard quarter: zilch. Port quarter…

Every muscle in her body stiffened. It was a mirage. A mirage. A long, white bit of nothing.

"Adam."

At least, that's what she thought she'd said. But there didn't seem to be enough breath in her body to push out the word. Her soul floated somewhere beyond her reach.

"Adam…"

The boat pitched, and Adam let out a whoop of joy. "Got one! Got one, get up here, you bugger…"

She whirled to find him pulling hard against a fish.

"Adam!" she screamed. "Look! I think I see land."

Adam turned toward her, and the line got yanked out of his hands. He lunged after it, but it disappeared into the water. "Damn."

She hopped up and down. "Look!"

Adam shook his head and came over. "It's a mirage."

No. No, it wasn't. It had shape, it had mass, and in the water around it… "Whitecaps," she said. "There *must* be land." Land, people, telephones, five-star restaurants and endless swimming pools…

"A tiny atoll," he said. "Maybe a reef…"

"We have to look."

Adam seemed to consider this for a decade or more. "Okay," he said at last, "but then we *will* be out of gas."

Out of gas, out of water — if they were going to die, let them at least die trying. Adam fired up the engine and pointed them at the vision on the water. Kalina stood at the bow of the boat, leaning out as far as she could go to watch as the shadow coalesced into the unmistakable shape of an island. After a few minutes she could make out vegetation, thick and dark green. She turned back to Adam, smiling in triumph.

He didn't look overjoyed. He looked deeply suspicious.

"Adam, look how big this place is!" she yelled over the engine as they got closer. "Maybe there's a settlement here."

"Maybe," he replied, but the concern remained on his face.

There was no sign of civilization on the shore they approached, no huts or docks or mooring balls that indicated people had ever lived on this island.

As the lifeboat drew closer, Adam cut the engine and let the waves carry them near the shore. The island was big, lush with vegetation. Large rocks jutted up from the shore, creating a sandy cover where they came aground.

Kalina jumped into the sand and let out a whoop for joy.

"Shh!" Adam said. "Careful."

"Careful?" she looked at him quizzically.

Adams' eyes scanned the brush and forest. "We don't know who is here. Maybe there's a settlement, but pirates sometimes use islands like this for hideouts."

Kalina's mouth snapped shut and she looked around fearfully. She'd never so much as seen the pirates that had taken over the yacht, and try as she might, she had a hard time picturing them. Her mind kept concocting crazy images of men in billowing shirts with gleaming swords, though she knew, rationally, they were nothing like that.

Adam stuffed all their empty water containers into his backpack. "Let's find some water and take a look around." She watched him slip something long and flat out of his pack and into the pocket of his pants.

"What's that?" she asked, as she followed him up the beach.

He gave her a long, dark look. "A knife."

Oh. Kalina shivered, despite the sun. No, the pirates that had killed the crew and taken her friends hostage were nothing like pirates in storybooks. Nothing like the Man in Black from her favorite movie. But this deckhand, who carried knives and never raised his voice and had kept them both alive for days and held her hand at night, then never spoke of it again — he was closer to the Dread Pirate Roberts than he had any right to be.

They picked their way through the vegetation, and Kalina winced as dead palm fronds and sharp shells sliced into her bare feet. She kept her face downturned as Adam went before her, trying to find soft, easy places to put her feet and noticed that he was limping.

"Are you all right?" she asked.

He paused in the bushes. "I… think I may have hurt my knee when I ran from the pirates. And I haven't tried to walk on it, really, in four days. Just stiff. I don't think it's broken or anything."

"Okay."

He looked back at her. "You shouldn't be walking around in bare feet."

"I'm not being left alone," she replied, but what she didn't add was, *You're all I've got.*

Adam glanced back at the boat on the beach and sighed. "You're right. I just — if you cut up your feet…"

"This morning I was going to die of dehydration," she pointed out. "Right now, a few cuts on my feet are not my greatest concern."

He gave another one of his endless, silent glances, then shrugged and started walking again.

They continued into the brush, but it only took Kalina about thirty seconds to notice that Adam had started stamping down the leaves, creating soft places for Kalina to step.

Eventually, they reached the trees, the canopy cover dark and cool compared to the blinding brightness of the sea. Kalina could hear birdsong and the buzzing of insects. Bright flowers bloomed from bromeliads and tall stalks shooting from vines on the ground. It was gorgeous, like something out of a picture postcard.

Having a Lovely Time, Wish You Were Here. All it needed was a five-star resort and this island would be a perfect paradise.

The ground sloped up, and Adam headed left, following some kind of signs she couldn't detect. She kept quiet, watching him looking at plants and feeling the rock. Is this what it was like if you were raised in the desert? Did you learn to find your way to water? After a few minutes walking, they ground went mushy, and moss covered the trees.

"There's water near here," was all he said.

A few moments later, they found it. A wide, green pool, thick with algae on the top. Kalina made a face. "We can't drink that."

"It's not ideal, no," Adam replied, and started picking his way around the perimeter of the pond. Near the other side, a wet stream trickled down the rock. "Look," he said, and held up one of the bottles to the trickle. The water that poured inside was clear.

"But we should still use our purification tablets, right?" she asked.

"To be safe," he said, eyeing the stream in its path up the rock. "But if it's coming from up there, I'm guessing there's a spring somewhere."

A spring! Kalina felt faint at the word. Cool, clear water to wash off the sun and salt and fear she'd been immersed in the last few days.

Adam dug his fingers into the rock and began to climb. She stood at the base of the incline, hands on her hips, as she watched him, his muscles straining against his filthy t-shirt, his face dark with intent and exertion. After a minute's hard climbing, he seemed to reach a plateau of some sort. He stood, brushed grit off his hands and looked around.

"Well?" she called up. "What do you see?"

Adam began to laugh. "Keep heading that way," he shouted to her. "I'll meet you there."

"Where?" she asked, but he disappeared around the side of the rock.

Frowning, Kalina picked her way through the muddy earth in the direction Adam had pointed, and found an easier-to-climb slope. With hands and feet, she managed to scramble up the side, and after about a fifty-foot climb, the ground fell away from her feet and she stared into a little stone grotto about six feet below. Water cascaded over the edge of the rock and into a deep, clear pool. Adam sat on a ledge, across the chasm, pulling off his shoes.

"Hey," he said, looking up at her as she approached. He dangled his toes down into the water.

She stared into their salvation. She'd never been so happy to see water in her life. All at once, something burst within her, an iridescent bubble of joy fizzier than any champagne, a rush stronger than any cocaine high.

She let out a whoop and leaped into the water below.

ten

ADAM'S HEART STOPPED WHEN KALINA JUMPED. A second later she splashed down into all the crystalline water, then surfaced, shook her dark hair out of her face and started to laugh.

"Come on in!" she yelled up to him. "The water's great!" She scooped up handfuls and poured it into her open mouth. "It's delicious."

"It's unfiltered," he warned her halfheartedly. He wasn't truly worried — this wasn't New Mexico, with livestock around to pollute the surface water. This pool was obviously spring-fed. The water was probably as pristine as any Kalina had paid for in fancy spas.

With a wet slap, Kalina's top hit the rocks by his feet. Her shorts followed.

"Get in, Adam!" She ducked beneath the water again and he saw her neon-panty-clad bottom rise up in the air before she kicked away.

He stood there, stupid, feeling the salt caking every crevice of his body. There was nothing he wanted more in the world than to go swimming in this glorious grotto with a half-naked Kalina St. Claire.

And that's why there was no way in hell he was going to do it.

Her hand closed around his ankle. "Get in here, Adam, or I'm going to pull you in."

He didn't look down, and covered by dropping the backpack to the ledge and pulling off his shirt. "Okay. But, um, back up. And don't look."

That laugh again. "What, you want me to turn around while you get undressed? Don't be a prude. I've been listening to you piss off the side of the boat for days."

He set his jaw and pulled off his shorts. "Fine." Good. Put him in his place. His sunbaked brain was starting to get enormously inappropriate ideas.

Adam dove in. The water was cool and sweet and glorious. He didn't even try to hold his breath as he went under, opening up and drinking it in. The salt melted from his skin and he surfaced, spluttering and sweeping his hair back and knowing that if he died that very second, he'd be happy.

For several minutes he just floated in that water, soaking it up like a desert tree, drinking it in and scrubbing all those days of salt and grime and blood off his skin. His knee ached, but he couldn't bring himself to care. He couldn't seem to bring himself to care about anything.

Across the grotto, Kalina was floating on her back, her breasts like little islands cresting the surface of the water. He ducked under again, closing his eyes against the image even as heat flooded his system and he grew hard. That would never do, to let her see. That was the kind of reaction she and her friends had been trying to provoke out of him all summer.

And it wasn't real, anyway. They were alive. They were alive, and that's why he felt this way, like some sort of crazy, near-death survival response.

When he'd gotten himself back under control, he emerged again, breathing hard.

Kalina paddled over, a grin the likes of which he'd never seen before splitting her features. "So now what?"

"Now what?" Adam echoed, half-delirious. He couldn't get enough. Enough water, enough cool shade, enough of her blinding smile.

"We're not going to die today, so now what?" She treaded water across from him, and the look she gave him was so…expectant… his dick stirred again.

Stop it, Adam thought at his unruly libido. *Stop looking at me like that,* he silently begged Kalina.

"I mean, should we gather food, make shelter, what?" she continued at last.

"Oh. Yeah." He nodded. How weird was it that Kalina was actually being the practical one? "Well, first we should make sure there's no one else here — like a fishing village."

"Or pirates," Kalina added. She took a deep breath. "How will we know the difference?"

"Guns," he answered. He honestly didn't know. Pirates weren't tricorn hats or skulls and crossbones. They were just men who wanted to kill you.

They scrubbed their clothes well, then laid them out on the rocks to dry. Kalina didn't seem in much of a hurry to get out of the water, but as soon as the initial adrenaline wore off, Adam was exhausted. He pulled himself up onto the ledge, in the shade, and checked his knee. His skin had split from impact with he deck of the *Palanquin*, a cut nearly four inches across, and bruising that radiated out over his swollen kneecap. But the cool water had brought some of the swelling down, and the salt sea air had helped him avoid any infection. A few days of rest, food, and water, and he should be fine.

He must have dozed off, as when his eyes opened again, the sun had slanted away from the grotto. He started immediately, jumping up. His clothes, next to him, were crusty and dry, and his pack was gone.

"Kalina?" he called, panic rising.

"Up here." She poked her head over the lip of the grotto. Her hair was dried and fluffed out all over her head, and she was wearing that purple shirt again, now wrinkled and draping stiffly around her. "I found coconuts. Man, they are hard to open."

She disappeared again and he heard a clunking sound start up. Lord only knew what she was using to try to open that coconut.

He groaned and pushed himself to his feet, grabbing his clothes and shoes again. The last thing he needed was her wandering off without him. And why had she let him fall asleep like that? They didn't know who else might be on the island.

"Hold on," he warned, dressing and climbing up the rock to meet her.

The sight that met his eyes had him sighing all over again. Kalina had the coconut gripped between her thighs and was chopping at it with the sharp edge of a Bible-sized rock. She'd already sheared away one side of the green exterior to reveal the fuzzy brown coconut beneath. He grimaced as she hacked away. "Be careful."

"You'd be surprised," she grunted, lifting the rock again and bringing it smack down on the scarred green coconut. "But I actually can"—*Smack!*—"do things for myself." *Smack!*

Yes, he actually would be surprised by that. He'd spent half the summer practically peeling grapes for this girl, and the past few days holding her hair back while she projectile vomited into the ocean.

With a satisfying thunk, the corner of the rock sank deep into the coconut pit.

"Ha!" Kalina jumped to her feet and held up the coconut, shaking the milk into her mouth. It splattered down her chin and throat, and she smacked her lips. "Wow, this is good. Have some." She thrust the nut in his face.

Adam took it and drank, mostly because it gave him something else to concentrate on than the sticky sheen of coconut milk running down Kalina's chin. The sweet, watery juice slid over his tongue — for that's what it was, he realized. Juice, even though he'd always heard it called milk.

Growing up on the desert ranch, coconut came in bags, dried and shredded for sprinkling on top of cakes. He'd never much cared for the flavor before, but maybe that's because he'd never had it fresh.

"I saw some berries, too," Kalina was saying, "but I didn't know what kind they were, so I didn't want to risk it. I know there's no such thing as a poisonous coconut."

"You shouldn't have gone off by yourself," he scolded.

"To be fair, you were dead to the world. I did try to wake you." She shrugged. "I'd rather you rested while we got the chance."

He saw his pack nearby and went to grab it, but it was heavier than expected.

"I went ahead and filled all the bottles we had with water," Kalina explained. She certainly had. She'd even retrieved the empty vodka bottle from the boat. "But I wasn't sure how to add the purification tablets, or if you even thought we should do it, since we were drinking it straight before."

Adam schooled the shock off his features before he dared to look at her. This was the spoiled, bitchy, helpless Kalina St. Claire? "Um, probably not. It's spring water."

She nodded. "That's what I figured."

Adam reached for one of the remaining rations. "We should probably eat and get back to exploring the island."

"Before dark," she said, agreeing. "So we still have time to make a shelter."

He blinked at her. "Make a shelter? Like, out of logs?"

"Yeah," she replied. "Or… palm fronds?" She was looking at him expectantly, like he somehow had all the answers, the definitive survive-on-a-desert-island plan.

"I have no idea," he said. "I've never been shipwrecked before."

"Technically, we aren't shipwrecked. I mean, the yacht is still out there somewhere."

He chuckled in spite of himself. "True. Not even our lifeboat is a wreck. We took decent care of it."

"No thanks to you. I was the one who found the tent."

"Indeed."

Kalina examined the coconut. "There's meat in here, if you can figure out a way to crack off the shell." She held it out. "Here."

"Yes, miss." The words came out automatically and he felt heat travel down his neck.

Kalina giggled. "Sorry. That wasn't meant to sound like a command."

"Wasn't it?"

She pursed her lips. "You're hardly on the clock anymore, Adam..." she trailed off and cocked her head at him thoughtfully. "Wait. What's your full name?"

"Adam Samuel Truman."

"Nice. I'm Kalina Noel St. Claire."

"Noel?" He smiled. "I have a sister named that."

She rolled her eyes. "Really? Was she also born on Christmas?"

"Christmas Eve. Actually, her name is Mary Noel, but my mom was Mary so we all just called her Noel."

"Who is 'we all'?"

He looked away as the faces of his family flashed before his eyes. Would he ever see them again? Where did they think he was right now? He'd written his parents about the trip to the Pacific, but hadn't gotten a response, like always. "I have a big family. Okay, let me take a whack at this coconut."

With that oh-so-smooth transition, he grabbed the coconut from her hands, wedged it in a crack in the rocks at the edge of the cliff, and started in on it again with the sharpened rock. Once he'd widened the crack enough to shove the edge of the rock inside, he wiggled it back and forth until it split halfway down the nut. He lifted the entire fruit and held it out to her. "Take the other side. Please."

She did and they pulled in opposite directions. The coconut split into two uneven pieces, and Kalina flew backwards, landing hard on her butt in the dirt.

"Oops, sorry," he said.

She gave him a look, then shook it off and cradled her piece of creamy white coconut innards.

"Let me get my knife, I'll carve you out a—" Adam cut off as Kalina buried her face in the crescent of coconut and started chomping.

Kalina St. Claire, who he'd never seen take to anything that wasn't alcohol or cocaine with so much gusto. Kalina St. Claire, who had practically bitten his head off for using a drill in her general vicinity last week, was now sitting cross-legged on a pile of dirt in week old clothes and looking happier than he'd ever seen her.

"What are you waiting for?" she asked him around a mouthful of coconut. There were white flecks all over her face.

"Sorry." He started eating. The flesh had an odd texture, like something between a nut and a celery stalk, and reminded him a lot of the shredded coating his mother baked with. He didn't like it as much as the juice. But as he looked at Kalina over the white and brown rim of the coconut, and watched her scrape every last bit of her half clean with her teeth and tongue, he realized that even acquired tastes were worth working for.

eleven

KALINA'S EYES FLUTTERED OPEN to the familiar sight of sunlight sifting through draped palm fronds. What was not familiar, however, was the sound of deep, even breathing coming from nearby. She shifted slightly on the tarp to see Adam, still fast asleep, a few feet away.

Thank goodness. For the first few days on the island he kept them to their rigid sleeping shifts. Even after she rebelled, arguing that they'd been around the island half a dozen times and there was no sign of anyone else there, he'd stayed up late into the night, and was always up before her, foraging in the woods or trying—and failing—to catch a fish in the lagoon. They probably should have been more careful with their one fishing line, back on the lifeboat.

Slowly, so she wouldn't wake him, Kalina slipped off the tarp and out of the tent flap, pushing aside the concealing palm fronds and stretching up into the morning. The light had turned the sea to lemonade, and the sky was that precious, silver-blue you only saw at dawn.

Were the dawns here more beautiful or had Kalina simply never appreciated dawn before?

She checked the tree first thing—one more mark on the calendar. Hard to believe it was already August. Her eyes began to burn as she wondered what was happening in the world outside. Were they still looking for her? What had happened to Bran and the others on the yacht?

No wasting water. Though it had been three weeks since Kalina had needed to worry about their water supply, she still used the mantra daily. It wasn't about the water— it was about crying over the things she couldn't change. All the crying in the world wasn't going to get them rescued, wasn't going to change the fact that pirates had boarded her boyfriend's yacht and killed the crew—at least the crew, and possibly everyone else. There was no way to know.

And nothing they could do about it. The important thing was that she and Adam were still alive, and they were going to stay that way until they were found. Swallowing back her tears, she headed to the latrine Adam had insisted on building, far away from their shelter.

Kalina supposed that if you were going to be shipwrecked, it was best to be shipwrecked with someone who knew how to build latrines and carried hunting knives and rope and first aid kits. She wasn't sure how they would have gotten through those first few days without his expertise and the supplies he kept in the backpack he called his "go-bag." Though Adam always claimed that he had no idea what he was doing, his actions spoke for themselves. If she were here with Bran, they'd probably have starved to death already.

Speaking of starving to death… Kalina grabbed the backpack and set off to find breakfast. Their foraging trips had taken them farther and farther into the interior of the island, stripping the palm trees of coconuts and growing more adventurous with other fruits. This was one area where Kalina's well-traveled background actually came in handy. Adam didn't know much about exotic fruits beyond bananas, but Kalina recognized mango, carambola, and breadfruit. They'd even found a papaya tree. It was all quite wonderful, but even Kalina knew they couldn't survive on fruit alone. She fell asleep at night dreaming of steaks and hamburgers. Even with Adam's careful rationing, they'd finished the lifeboat's supply of beef jerky last week.

There wasn't much that Kalina could contribute to their survival — she was a mess with a knife and shelter building, her hands had blistered within minutes when trying to dig the latrine, and she'd gaped at Adam whenever he scaled rocks or trees like a monkey.

"There aren't a lot of trees to climb in Manhattan," she explained to him. Hell, she rarely even entered buildings without elevators.

"There aren't a lot of trees in the desert, either," Adam had replied. "But I did climb lots of rocks."

Still, she could pick low hanging fruit and fill water bottles, and so she always made sure to do both, every day. Adam was building shelters and starting fires and all the other stuff he'd apparently picked up in whatever backwoods desert ranch where he'd grown up. She should do something as well.

The only problem was, there wasn't a whole lot of fruit left. As the sun rose higher in the cloudless sky, she started climbing the island's main outcropping, heading to a new section of jungle in hopes of discovering a fresh supply of fruit trees. Up here, cool morning breezes wafted the ends of her hair and made her nightshirt billow out around her. As she picked her way across the jagged rocks, she marveled at how hard and calloused her feet had grown in the last week. Tiny dots of color in the center of each toe were all that remained of her careful pedicure, and each of her fingernails was broken and ragged from scrambling over rocks or scraping at coconuts.

How odd. Once, in Manhattan, Kalina had canceled a date because of a broken nail. She didn't want to be seen at anything other than her best. What would the world think of her now, running around a desert island in an old silk nightshirt and a pair of cutoffs, foraging for fruit like some kind of cavewoman?

You could practically see the Movie of the Week already. *Shipwrecked Heiress. Debutante Gone Wild.*

Of course, in the movie, she'd probably be rescued by some handsome sea captain, or her companion on the island would be a secret prince, not a college student who could barely hide his disgust for her.

Kalina couldn't think back to their first day on the island without going maroon with humiliation. The moment they found the grotto, and she knew they'd survive, she'd been filled with overwhelming elation, a joy that couldn't be contained in words, that couldn't be satisfied with a dive off a cliff, or a swim in a lake, or a simple smile from the cute boy at her side. She wanted to be *alive*—to *feel* alive, after days of wondering if she was going to die.

It seemed so natural to her, to take off her clothes and encourage him. Any other male of her acquaintance would have taken that hint and jumped her bones. But what did Adam do? He'd ignored her advances, lectured her about water-borne illnesses, and fallen asleep on a rock.

He must think she was some sort of crazy slut. He must find her disgusting. The man preferred cuddling up to a slimy piece of granite than the woman the *New York Post* had once mistaken for Cindy Crawford, much to Kalina and her friends' amusement and the model's—or at least her agent's—ire.

Now, she wasn't even sure she could pass for a convincing Blue-Lagoon-era Brooke Shields. And if Adam's opinion was anything to go by, her shipwreck chic…wasn't.

Kalina crested the top of the outcrop and scanned the canopy below, looking for coconut palms that may have escaped their notice on former foraging trips. So far, they'd been lucky, but she didn't know if there were enough trees on this island to keep them fed, nor what kind of nutritional problems they'd start having on a mostly-coconut diet.

Or how long any of this could be sustained. Building a latrine might come in handy, if it turned out they did end up getting dysentery or some other crazy disease.

No, there'd be no romantic movie made of her situation. And she supposed it didn't really matter, in the scope of first surviving and then getting rescued at all. She'd broached the topic of rescue with Adam precisely once.

He had grunted, and looked away, which Kalina now understood to mean it wasn't something he wanted to talk about. Just like he hadn't wanted to talk about the dead crew, or his childhood, or his favorite pop songs, or his five movies he'd take to a desert island.

"I don't understand," he'd said. "We don't even have power. We couldn't show them."

"Fine," she'd replied, throwing her hands up in defeat. "Top five books."

Forty-five minutes later, Kalina figured she could keep up passably well in a graduate level seminar on magical realism. And she wasn't exactly sure what she'd learned about Adam's romantic tastes, given books with titles like *Love in the Time of Cholera.* She'd heard of it, of course, but… well, reading wasn't exactly Kalina's strong suit.

And when she hung out with Adam, she wasn't sure she had a strong suit. The things she'd valued — her ability to spot a knock-off at fifty yards, her withering glare, her skill at applying mascara without a mirror—none of those were the slightest bit useful here on an island at the edge of the world. She'd spent her adult life to date snapping her fingers and watching the male side of the species fall in line to be with her.

It had all been a waste of time.

Adam could make fire out of flint. He could tell time by the angle of the sun. He could scale a palm tree in fifteen seconds. He'd kept them alive on the boat, and he was doing a pretty good job here on the island.

On the *Palanquin*, she'd thought he was cute. That first day, in the grotto, she'd decided he was fuckable. Now, she realized how insanely inadequate both of those impressions were. Adam Truman was a capital-M *Man*, the likes of which she had never in her life dated, had barely even met. The longer she spent with him, the more impressed she was.

And he thought she was the scum of the Earth.

As she rounded a boulder, she saw movement out of the corner of her eye, and froze.

Three little goats, their hair shaggy, their horns hardly more than stubs on their heads. They were grazing, calm, their heads down. She backed up, afraid of startling them, as her mind raced with possibilities.

She could grab a big rock. No, she should go back down and get Adam. He probably knew how to kill a goat. Wait, would she really kill a goat? What if it was just the three of them? Poor goats!

No, Kalina, don't be stupid. They needed protein and iron to survive. If there were three goats here, there had to be more… somewhere? Right?

Adam. Kalina nodded, mostly to herself. She should get Adam.

She raced back down the slope, wincing a bit as her feet caught the edges of rocks and gravel. Adam, Adam, Adam. He'd know what to do.

Back on the beach, she padded through the sand and up to the tent, dropping the empty pack by the flaps as she rushed inside and knelt by his head.

"Adam." She touched his shoulder, a mass of muscle bronzed dark by the Pacific sun. "Get up."

His eyes shot open, those stormy, sea-tossed eyes. "What's wrong?"

"Nothing." She smiled. "I found some goats."

He didn't say another word, just got to his feet and slipped his clothes on, shoved his feet into his shoes, then grabbed his knife and a rope. "Take me to them."

As they crossed the beach again, Kalina peppered him with questions. "What are you going to do?" "Have you butchered animals before? "How many do you think there are?" "Can I help?"

At this last one, he stopped on the trail and turned to look at her. "Yeah. Stay out of the way. Goats have horns."

Kalina's mouth snapped shut. Wasn't he even excited?

Up on the outcropping, Kalina pointed out the boulder where she'd seen the goats. Adam crept over and took a peek around the other side. "There are five."

"Five!" Kalina whispered, excited. "Five is better than three! I feel better about killing one if there's five."

He gave her a dark look. "More doesn't make it easier for one to die."

Kalina took a step back. "I mean… there will be more left. For later."

But Adam didn't respond, just walked a few paces to a twisted tree and threw his rope over, tying a little noose on the end.

"Are you going to hang it?" she whispered.

"I'm going to bleed it," he replied. When he was done with the knots, he turned back to the animals, studying them in a way Kalina wasn't comfortable with examining too closely.

"That one," he said at last. "With the black face. It's a juvenile male, so it should be good eating, and you won't have to worry that it's pregnant or nursing a kid."

Kalina swallowed, suddenly sick to her stomach. "A kid?"

But it was too late. Adam had jumped out on the herd, falling square on the back of the little goat and clasping his arms about its neck.

The other animals scattered, bleating, as Adam's chosen goat bucked and grunted. Adam yanked the animal's head in the air. She saw the flash of a knife.

The beast kicked out then and Adam lost his grip on the knife. It went skittering across the rocks.

"Dammit!" he shouted, and Kalina looked from the knife to the struggling pair.

"Do you want me to get it?" she asked.

"You think?" The animal bucked again, whirling over the rocks and kicking wildly. Kalina darted around the two of them and retrieved the knife, but didn't see any way to get it to Adam, who looked like he was hanging on for dear life.

She'd never before heard a goat scream, but this one was screaming. Kalina felt hot and cold all at once. Adam wrestled the animal to the ground.

"The knife!" he barked at her, and whipped it out of her hands. She looked away.

There was a sickening thunk, and the goat's noises gurgled away. When Kalina had the guts to look again, Adam was already dragging the dead animal over to the tree and hanging it up by its hind legs. Its throat was slit wide open, and a bloody trail scarred the rocks. Adam's hands were dark red past his elbows and his face and shirt were spattered with gore.

Kalina pressed a fist to her mouth as Adam hoisted the goat up and blood poured from the open wound.

"Are you going to throw up?" he asked without turning his head from his work.

He'd killed a goat for her. There were scrapes and scratches all over his arms, and he was covered in blood and he'd killed a goat for her. It was horrific and disgusting and absolutely necessary for their survival.

Kalina took a deep breath. "No." One more. "How can I help?"

She was done staying out the way.

twelve

KALINA ST. CLAIRE HELPED ADAM drag the
carcass of the goat back to the beach. Kalina St. Claire
gathered driftwood for the smoke pit while Adam
removed the head and forelegs. Kalina St Claire
poured buckets of salt water across the bottom of the
lifeboat to evaporate in the sun, then brushed the
salts that remained into a hollowed out coconut shell.

All that was difficult, if not impossible, for Adam
to believe. But it was when Kalina St. Claire sat there
and watched as he skinned the goat, then asked if she
could try her hand at the knife that he started to
wonder if maybe the both of them had gone a little
bit mad.

She was awful at it, of course. Skinning an animal
isn't as easy as those homesteading pioneers made it
seem, no matter how much his father would try to
beat their lessons into Adam and his brothers. But
Adam couldn't seem to get enough of watching her
try, of seeing her swipe her tangled hair out of her

face and stick out her tongue to concentrate on the movements of her knife hand, of the way she tugged in vain to yank the skin away from the flesh of the animal he had killed. Every clumsy, awkward movement hit him deep in the gut, a crude if satisfying sensation Adam figured men had been getting since the first cave hunter had dragged the first saber-toothed goat back to his woman.

The rational, college student part of Adam thought he was disgusting.

Other parts didn't bother to think.

"I don't know if I'll ever look at meat the same way again," Kalina said, after about fifteen minutes of effort. She looked distastefully at the progress she'd made. "Poor goat."

"Maybe that's a good thing," said Adam. "We'd be less inclined to waste food, I think, if we knew about the suffering we caused to get it." But right now, he wasn't thinking about suffering. He felt high, powerful, the way he never had after butchering an animal on the farm. Even when he'd shot coyotes or other predators on the ranch, he hadn't felt so…so…

Primal.

"Spoken like a true philosopher." She handed back the knife.

"This isn't philosophy studies," he replied, as he took over, expertly shearing a line down the animal's hindquarter. No. Right now he was anything but a philosopher. No wonder they called it bloodlust. He hadn't felt so out of control since their first day on the island. "This is me growing up eating animals my little sister had named."

"Noel?"

Adam swallowed, as the image of his pigtailed sister rose up in his mind, chasing away all his baser instincts. "I have a lot of little sisters."

Kalina hugged her knees to her chest and rested her chin on them. "Really? How many?"

He didn't need this to turn into a freak show. He shook his head and concentrated on his work.

"I always wanted siblings," she went on, to the back of his head. "I think, maybe, if I'd had them, it would have been easier when my parents died."

Right, the helicopter crash.

"I mean, my grandfather lost his daughter, and that was its own kind of hell, I'm sure. But I was seven—"

Seven. Adam's knife hand shook.

"—and they were my parents, my whole little nuclear family. I was alone."

Maybe there *was* a difference. Adam wouldn't know. He'd been far from alone, and it still felt like a black hole had opened up in his heart.

"My brother died when I was sixteen." His mouth formed the words and spoke them before Adam could think better of it. "Joshua."

"I'm sorry."

"He was a little kid." Sweet, smiling Joshua, who tagged along behind him everywhere. There were six siblings between Adam and Joshua, but it didn't make a difference to them. It had been Adam who'd taught Joshua to read, to ride a bike, to do his chores. "He was seven." Way too young for anything traumatic, just as Kalina had been too young to lose her whole world.

"What happened?"

Adam shrugged. "He got sick."

Three words that didn't come anywhere close to telling the story. Joshua had gotten sick, all right, but it was his parents who had killed him. They refused to get the boy treated, trusting that God would find a way for him.

Joshua died, and everything the Trumans had raised Adam to believe about their way of life died with him. For a long time, Adam wasn't sure who he hated more, his parents or God, but he was damn sure he was going to get away from both of them.

College, St John's, Annapolis—to him it was an escape.

He tugged at remnants of the skin. His skills were rusty, but not totally gone.

"How many other brothers and sisters do you have?"

His head snapped up. "Does it matter?"

Her eyes were wide. "Oh. No, I'm… that's not what I—" She looked away, down into the dirt. "So that's what you meant. About the goats."

Adam's heart pounded. He supposed she was right. He hadn't even thought of it. Why was she even listening to him?

"Twelve," he mumbled. "I have twelve. The last two I've never even met." The twins, Patience and Paul.

She didn't whistle through her teeth at the number, didn't express outrage over his lack of visits to the old homestead. He guessed, what with their being trapped on a desert island, the point was probably moot anyway.

"I haven't seen them in a while," he said, as he finished skinning the goat and laid the skin out over the line he'd strung between coconut palms. "And I'm an enormous disappointment to them."

She chuckled. "I have a really hard time believing that."

He sliced open the animal's belly. "I assure you, it's the truth. Okay, this next part is gross, but I think we'll be glad to keep as many organs as we can. You have the tarp all laid out?"

"Yes. Adam, I think your parents would be really proud to see how you've been able to use the things they taught you to keep us alive, on the ocean, here on the island…"

He began unwinding the intestines, hoping the smell might drive her away, bring out the bitchy, superior Kalina St. Claire he knew. Maybe he should tell her how she was wrong. About everything. He seemed to remember she hated that.

And she *was* wrong. His parents didn't give a shit if he survived or not. He was lost to them anyway, headed to Hell, so it made no difference if he was already there. They'd have half a dozen things to say about the way he'd conducted himself, and most would be regarding the fact that he'd never have found himself trapped on this island with what they'd no doubt call a godless whore if he hadn't gone off into secular society in the first place.

Also, he hated how Kalina seemed to think he had the answers. So he could butcher a goat. Anyone who grew up on a farm could butcher a goat. It didn't make him Survival Sam. He had no idea what the probability was of someone from the outside spotting this little atoll. Nor did he know if the rainy season was going to come in and sink them all. He'd spent his entire childhood awaiting the Apocalypse. It hadn't exactly prepared him for anything except the worst.

They laid out organs, one by one, on the tarp.

"I say we cook the organs and eat them first. I don't know how pancreas dries, honestly. I know you can dry liver, but we're probably better off eating that fresh, too. And anything we don't eat we should bury."

Kalina stood with her hands on her hips, studying the meats. "How long do you think this will last?"

"Tough to tell how long we can keep the meat until it goes rancid. But with smoking and drying and salting…" he trailed off, doing the calculations in his head. "If we can preserve most of it, then a few months."

Kalina's whole face changed when she smiled, her burnt brown skin glowing against her straight white teeth. She went from imperious queen to sweet saint, like an illustration of the Virgin Mary in his mother's Bible.

No, actually, nothing at all like the Virgin Mary. Too earthy and raw and alive and dear God, the way she was looking at him right now, like he'd hung the moon…

"Months," she repeated, awed. "On one goat."

"It'll probably go rancid."

"Or it won't." Her hand grazed his shoulder and the touch buzzed like a live wire. Adam's nerve endings went wild.

They never touched. Not anymore. That first night, off the boat, when they'd set up the lifeboat's tent as a shelter beneath the palms on the beach, they'd crawled inside and he'd lain there, beside her, an awkward foot and a half away, and thought about how easy it would be to just pull her into his arms and kiss her and rejoice in being alive and on dry land. So ridiculously easy and justified that he'd shoved his hands beneath his body to keep from grabbing her like it was his right.

He heard the sound of skin against the tarp, the scrabble of her fingers reaching for him, to grasp his fingers like they had so many nights on the boat. But he couldn't risk touching any part of her.

And so they hadn't touched. Not in weeks.

His blood boiled beneath his skin. His fingers itched. There was an animal on this beach all right, but it wasn't the one he'd butchered.

"I know you're always waiting for the other shoe to drop, but let's just take a second and appreciate what we did."

"You appreciate it," he said. "I'm going to go wash the blood off." He practically sprinted down the beach, hard as a rock, his balls aching between his legs. He shed his clothes like old skin and dove beneath the waves as her name became a heartbeat in his head. *Kalina, Kalina, Kalina.*

There were rocks here at this end of the beach. Tall, concealing rocks where Adam could hide and spit into his hand and wrap it around his throbbing dick and take care of business alone.

He was sick. All summer, those girls on the yachts had been shoving their suntan-oiled breasts in his face and tossing their perfectly permed hair and begging for him to take advantage of them, and when did he decide to go mad with lust? When he saw one in a dirty old nightshirt with sunburnt skin pick up a knife and utterly fail to skin a goat.

Kalina. Her windswept hair and full breasts swinging beneath that skimpy little chemise. The tiny moans she made in her sleep. The way she relished every drop of coconut milk and licked her fingers after. The looks she gave him when he climbed a tree or moved a log, like he was the only man on the face of the planet—

"Ah!" The orgasm was swift and almost painful in its intensity. He pulsed into the surf, then slumped against the rock, hanging his head in shame, the way he'd done when he was younger and still believed God would punish him for jerking off.

But it was better this way. Better to fantasize about touching her than make a mess of things with the last person he might ever see alive.

"Dammit," he growled. "Get a hold of yourself. Remember, this is Kalina St. Claire."

It didn't work though, because Adam was beginning to suspect that he'd never known who Kalina St. Claire was at all.

thirteen

KALINA WAS DRUNK. The goat pancreas had turned into alcohol in the fire. It was the only explanation for the way she felt, full and sleepy and lightheaded. Laughter seeped out of her like molasses and she leaned back into the sand, staring into the flames of the bonfire and sighing in pleasure.

Adam had been all business when he got back from his swim that morning. They'd spent the rest of the day slicing every scrap of meat off the goat and setting up the smoker and trying to gather as much salt as they could. The meat would go bad quickly in the humid island air, Adam had warned, so it was imperative to try and preserve it right away.

As the sun dipped low in the sky, she'd rebelled, saying they were having barbecue for dinner that night. She'd been saving their best looking coconut shells, so they actually had plates and cups—of sorts—and Adam's camp silverware from his pack, and a forked twig they'd found in the forest. Adam, of course, had insisted she use the real silverware.

Who knew goat pancreas was so very delicious? Who knew that after a long, hard day of work, the simple act of lying before a fire and making dumb jokes, dead sober, would be her favorite activity in the entire world? The southern stars twinkled above them, and the moon made a silver path across the sea.

Adam was worried about the smoker. He was always so worried. She wished there were something she could do, but he was the only one who knew how things worked, so it wasn't like she could argue with him when he claimed that he wasn't sure he'd set up the fire right.

"It's not inconceivable that we're actually burning that goat instead of smoking it."

"Inconceivable," she mocked, affecting a drunken Spanish accent. "You keep using that word. I do not think it means what you think it means."

He looked at her as if she were crazy. And maybe she was.

"It's from a movie," she explained sheepishly. "*The Princess Bride.*"

He gave a little shake of his head, but a smirk ghosted across his face. "Not familiar with it."

Kalina flopped back in the sand. "Oh, it's my favorite movie. It's all about princesses and farm boys and pirates…"

Oh. *Oh.* She sat up.

"Not real pirates. Movie pirates."

"Of course." He dug his toes into the sand. "Okay, tell me more."

So she did. In fact, she ended up acting out the best parts, like the battle of wits the man in black and the Sicilian challenge each other to.

"So they live in a fairy tale country, but they talk about Sicily and Australia?" Adam looked at her skeptically. "This sounds like a very strange story."

"It's the best story. The best love story."

"The princess and the pirate?"

"No," Kalina laughed. "The grandfather and the little boy." She drizzled sand across her legs. "Well, the princess and the pirate too. Or the farm boy. Whatever. The fact that they never gave up on each other, no matter how long it took before they saw each other again. True love."

Across the fire, Adam nodded slowly. "You believe in true love?"

"Yes." She buried her fingers into the sand, as if seeking to hold on to the earth itself. "My parents loved each other very much, before they died." And they'd loved her, and her grandfather…

Adam said nothing and she pulled her hands into her lap, feeling the grit on her fingers between her skin and the ring on her left hand. Her mother's wedding ring.

"What?" she asked nervously. "Don't you believe in true love? Your parents are still married, right?"

"They are still married."

"That's not an answer."

He shrugged. "I don't think you want my answer."

"So that's a no."

He was silent for a long moment. "My family believes in a certain way of life. If you don't live the way they want, they don't want to have anything to do with you. I wonder, if that farm boy had become a murderous pirate, if the princess really would have forgiven him."

Kalina thought about that for a moment. She couldn't imagine ever losing her parents' love. Then again, her parents were dead, her grandfather uninvolved. If they'd been around to see what she was making of herself, would they have cut her out of their lives too? Maybe there really was no such thing as true love, no hope for Buttercup and her pirate.

Adam spoke up again. "And you and Bran? True love?"

Kalina gaped. "…Bran? Oh, wow. No. Adam, I hate his guts."

"What?" He narrowed his eyes at her. "But… he was your boyfriend."

"He was—he is"—she wouldn't let herself believe that Bran had been murdered—"an enormous asshole. He cheated on me with a stewardess."

"So you knew about that."

"So everyone knew about it, you mean?" She rolled her eyes. "Jesus. How embarrassing."

"Embarrassing for you. Disastrous for Anna."

Kalina supposed she deserved that. Although, Anna was better off, not being on board when the real pirates came.

"Although it did save her life, in a way," Adam added, to her shock.

She swallowed, and waited a moment before she spoke again. "Do you know why I was in the lifeboat that night?"

He regarded her through the flames. "I kind of stopped questioning the things you passengers did at night. It was easier that way."

"He hit me." There. She said it. Adam's face was cast in shadow, so she couldn't see his response. "In bed that night. I didn't want to be on the same boat as him, let alone the same room." She looked down at the sand, at the way the white drifts had turned gold and orange in the firelight.

A shadow fell across her thighs, and his voice drifted in, low and comforting. "I'm sorry." He'd moved across the fire to be closer to her, but was still a respectable foot or so away. Just like every night in the tent.

She shrugged. "I guess he saved my life too."

"Yeah." Adam's fingers moved through the sand between them. This was as late as they'd stayed up since getting here. "I spent years fighting my instincts to hit. My parents had this saying: spare the rod, spoil the child. I was used to being beat with a switch for any misbehavior at all. When I got older, I was expected to inflict the same punishments on my younger siblings."

Kalina's throat closed up as she thought of young Adam being forced to beat the even younger Joshua. The one whose name he could barely say without crying.

"The first time I took a switch to one of my brothers, I threw up," he confessed, his focus on the fire. "But I didn't know what else to do. I'd never been taught any alternative. I'm not saying he was right—"

"I know you're not," she reached for his hand, but he scooted it out of her way. She tucked her hand between her knees, seeking the heat he'd denied her. "I guess we can only work with the tools we have."

Didn't that explain why she was utterly useless at everything? After her grandfather had gotten sick when she was fourteen, not a soul in the universe cared what she did or how she fared. She'd been given no tools at all, at the most vulnerable age in a girl's life. No wonder she was such a fuck up.

"Okay." She shook off the gloom. No more talk of abuse. "Your turn to act out a movie."

"I can't."

"A book."

He shook his head.

"A poem, then, Adam! Come on, let's get a little culture around here. A man cannot live on goats alone."

He smiled at that. "Okay. You need a love story?"

"Those are the best kind."

"I only know one," he warned her.

"If it's a good one, it doesn't matter."

The storm in his eyes came ever closer. "Oh, it's the best one." He took a deep breath, then began to recite:

I slept but my heart was awake.
Listen! My beloved is knocking:
"Open to me, my sister, my darling,
My dove, my flawless one.
My head is drenched with dew,
my hair with the dampness of the night."

At first, Kalina wanted to snicker. Seriously, *my dove*? If anyone ever called her "my dove" she'd slam the door in his face. But then Adam went on, slowly, carefully, his tone ripe with the meaning behind the archaic words, and all desire to laugh was drowned in another desire entirely.

> *I have taken off my robe— must I put it on again?*
> *I have washed my feet—must I soil them again?*
> *My beloved thrust his hand through the latch-opening;*
> *my heart began to pound for him.*

Her lips parted and her heart began to pound. It was in no way a *latch-opening* that the speaker—or Adam—was talking about.

> *I arose to open for my beloved,*
> *and my hands dripped with myrrh,*
> *my fingers with flowing myrrh,*
> *on the handles of the bolt.*

Kalina took one shuddering breath, then another. Her mouth was dry. Her story had been a funny one, with giants and eels and rodents of unusual size. This was porn. Weird and old-fashioned, but also beautiful and heartbreaking and shamelessly erotic. As Adam kept going, things went poorly for the girl in the poem, after the wonderful bit where she opened her *myrrh-dripping door* for her lover, and she ended up beaten by the men of the watch. But she never forgot her love.

> *Daughters of Jerusalem, I charge you—*
> *if you find my beloved,*
> *what will you tell him?*
> *Tell him I am faint with love.*

Silence fell, and the fire crackled, and Adam just looked at her and the storm in his gaze threatened to swallow her whole.

At last, she found her voice. "What poem is that?"

"The Song of Songs," he replied. "It's in the Bible."

"There is no way," Kalina said, breathless, "that is from the Bible."

He chuckled. "Trust me, Kalina. That passage was my life when I was twelve."

Dear God in heaven—no pun intended. She tried to imagine what it had been like growing up in a world where the closest a hormonal pubescent boy could get to porn was hot Bible passages. No wonder he wasn't impressed by Stevie's seduction techniques, or her own. He had come of age to erotica that had survived for millennia.

Kalina was starting to piece together enough of Adam's life to make a picture: rural ranch in the desert, super religious parents, and apparently a rejection of all of that when he'd gone to college to be a philosophy major. Or maybe not all of it.

"Are you a virgin?" She clapped her hand over her mouth, feeling the grit of sand against her teeth. Stupid. *Stupid.* Maybe she *was* drunk on pancreas.

He glared at her. "I said, when I was *twelve.*"

That wasn't, Kalina noted, an answer. "You know I'm not a virgin," she pointed out.

He didn't even dignify that with an answer.

"I was just wondering," she explained. "I mean, you quote sexy Bible passages at me, I thought maybe you believed in saving yourself."

"My first year in college, I didn't know what to do," he said abruptly. "I had left my home, my family, and everything they'd raised me to believe. I thought if I was going to reject it, I'd reject it all. I grew my hair long and drank and smoked and slept around. If I could have found a Communist Party in Annapolis, I probably would have joined it."

She tried to imagine that Adam—hippie, drunk, slutty Adam—and failed. "How long did that phase last?"

"Phase. Good choice of words. A year. I got it all out of my system that year."

"And since then?"

He snorted and shook his head. "I have girlfriends, if that's what you're getting at. I'm not a monk just because I didn't fuck any of your friends on the yacht."

That crude word out of his mouth twisted her insides in a strange and not unpleasant way. He wasn't wearing his shirt right now—it was drying near the fire, and the curves of his muscles were etched in gold and black by the light of the flames. She had the oddest desire to run her tongue along the groove of his biceps.

"You know what's weird?" he asked. "How we're all so obsessed with virginity. I thought it was just some religious purity thing growing up, but even out in the secular—I mean, even out in the real world, it was like every girl I slept with wanted to tell me how she lost her virginity, and to know how I lost mine. Like it was the only sexual encounter that mattered."

"Well, it does tend to stick in one's mind." She hugged her knees to her chest.

"It didn't for me. I was eighteen and drunk and at a party. She had brown hair and a birthmark on her left breast."

Kalina inhaled, sharp and sudden, at the image of Adam fumbling around at a party with that girl. It was a clearer picture than she had of some of her sexual partners. "Sounds like you remember just fine."

"I didn't love her," he said. "I didn't even know her name. I may not be as experienced as you, but I do know that sex is better with groundwork."

"Not always," she said softly. "I knew the man I lost my virginity to, and it was awful."

Adam fell silent. "Shit. I'm sorry."

She shrugged, looking into the fire. "It's okay. It was a long time ago."

Kalina had been fourteen, and he was the father of one of her friends from school. Her grandfather had just had his first stroke, and he'd been nice enough to drive her home to Connecticut from the hospital in Manhattan, to dismiss the servants and see her to her room.

He'd fixed her a drink, to help her nerves, he said, and then another, because he said he liked the way it made her blush, and somehow they'd started talking. She told him about a boy she had a crush on in school, who wouldn't give her the time of day, and he told her that boy was crazy, because Kalina was beautiful, so beautiful, so much more beautiful than his greedy bitch of an ex-wife or his gold-digging mistress. She was so soft, and so young, and so tight—he claimed—later that night when he took off her clothes and humped away on top of her.

Kalina had started crying after, afraid of what her friend would do if she found out.

"My mistake," the man had said as he buckled his pants. "I thought you were a woman. Apparently you're nothing but a stupid little girl."

She'd never told a soul. She'd stopped speaking to her friend. And she'd decided she was never going to be a little girl again. Little girls' parents died, their grandfathers forgot how to walk and speak and eat. But women could make men wild with a flick of their hair or a flash of their skin.

"Don't you worry," Kalina said to Adam, straightening. "I've had plenty of good sex since then."

"With Bran."

She made a face. No, not with Bran. But there had been a few guys in there, young, hot, and desperate to please her for her money. They were good, at least until they started asking for more than she wanted to give. At least until they disappeared off the face of the Earth. No one ever stayed, even if she wasn't holding out for true love.

"Ugh," she said instead. "How did we even get on this topic of conversation?"

"You started it."

"No!" She flicked sand at him. "You did, with your dirty poem."

He looked hurt. "It's a beautiful poem."

"It is," she agreed. Their eyes met, and for an endless moment, they just stared. Kalina forgot to breathe. She forgot she even needed to breathe.

I am faint with love.

If Adam so much as moved a millimeter in that moment, Kalina would have jumped his bones.

But he was still as a statue glowing bronze in the firelight, and together they sat like ancient ruins on a forgotten beach, and didn't speak, and didn't touch, and kept their secrets silent and safe.

It was Kalina who looked away first, who stood and brushed the sand off her bare thighs. "I think I'm going to go to bed." A few steps back from the fire, she stopped. "Do you want to come with me?"

Was that an invitation? Or a plea?

His face was in shadow with the fire burning bright around it, creating a halo out of his shaggy hair. "I'm going to check on the smoker. Make sure we've got enough fuel for the night."

"Oh," she said. "Okay." She turned toward the island's dark heart, hardly knowing what she looked like in that moment, but willing to do anything so Adam couldn't see the disappointment on her face.

In the tent, she took off her shorts and bikini bottoms, and lay down on the mat. She'd forgotten what mattresses felt like, and the touch of silk sheets.

Sex is better with groundwork.

She knew exactly what he meant, and it had nothing to do with her experiences at fourteen. Adam meant knowing your partner, what they liked, what made them tick—what made them sigh and groan and scream. And Kalina would bet Adam was *very* thorough in that regard—at least, after he'd gotten done sowing his wild oats that first year. He was meticulous in everything he did, on the *Palanquin*, on the island. If he wanted to devastate a woman in bed, she was quite sure he had the attention span to do so.

I slept, but my heart was awake.

Kalina felt that biblical girl's pain. Her mind held tight to Adam's words, to the way he made *myrrh* sound like a dirty promise and *beloved* like the sweetest of nothings.

That was the problem, she realized. She could have all the sex in the world, but she'd never been anyone's beloved.

There, beneath the sand-scarred flaps of their red lifeboat tent, Kalina was filled with an ancient and unquenchable ache, and though she waited for hours, Adam did not come to bed, and nothing else could soothe her to sleep.

fourteen

WEEKS PASSED ON THE ISLAND, and the only way Adam knew was by the marks on the tree, the dwindling supply of dried goat jerky, and the percentage of *The Princess Bride* he now knew by heart, despite never having seen it. He knew that the farm boy said "As you wish" instead of "I love you," he had memorized the rules of the fire swamp, and he could almost envision the dreadful life-sucking machine where the hero was tortured.

Adam realized now that this must have been the film she was watching that horrible day on the boat when she'd yelled at him. Sword fights and grandfathers. To listen to Kalina, it was the best movie ever made. Since she'd watched so many more than Adam had, he was hardly in a position to disagree. She made it sound pretty wonderful.

And even if it was total dreck, Adam could have spent hours listening to Kalina's reenactments, the way her face would grow bright and animated, her awful attempts at British and Spanish accents, her fake swordplay across the sand. She loved the film, and that was enough for him.

His own attempts at providing entertainment weren't nearly so successful. Most of the things Adam had memorized over the years were Bible verses, and though the Old Testament stories were riveting enough, he never did return to the Song of Songs.

That way lay madness.

According to the calendar, they'd hit September, the date that marked what would have been the end of the *Palanquin's* journey. The day broke in a rare gloom, a haze of clouds across the sea. Adam slept in that morning, and when he got up, he found Kalina standing thigh deep in the waves off their beach, her eyes scanning the horizon.

He joined her in the surf. Once upon a time, he had counted down the days until he'd never have to see her again. Now that date had arrived, and he could hardly imagine a moment without her.

"Do you think they're all right?" she surprised him by asking. "Bran and the others?"

"Yes," he lied, for the truth was, he had no idea. On one hand, surely if the pirates had planned to murder the passengers, wouldn't they have done it as quickly as they had with the crew? On the other, he had no idea if attempts at ransom went well, or what price the people on the *Palanquin* might have been forced to pay for Adam—and Kalina's—escape.

"Do you think they are looking for us?"

"Yes." Another lie. Chances were, every soul on the *Palanquin* was dead, and the world probably thought that meant him and Kalina, too. There was enough in cash and jewels on the boat to make the takeover worth the pirates' time without messing around with ransom.

Still, he and Kalina had left signs on the island, in case of a passing plane or boat. Every beach and bare, rocky outcropping was decorated with the word HELP in carefully arranged letters five yards long, in hopes that they might be spotted from the air. At four different locations along the shore, they'd readied piles of wood smeared with goat fat, in case they needed to light quick bonfires at the sight of a ship.

But Adam knew how slim their chances were. The island was a tiny speck in a vast ocean, and even scanning the sea twenty-four hours a day—which they didn't do—was unlikely to result in anything.

Kalina could envision rescue. Adam would spend his energies thinking about how to make a future on the island. Though they hadn't yet explored the entire interior of the jungle, he'd done his best to count the goats—there were six now, after their slaughter, which made him think they were probably a somewhat recent addition to the island, as they'd neither caused major damage to the vegetation nor bred to unsustainable numbers. And if they were recent, did that mean there might be another island, not so far away? Maybe an island where people did live?

The best thing to do would be to round them up and use their offspring for a renewable food source, the females for milk. But then they'd be responsible for feeding even more mouths.

Kalina might believe he had all the answers, but this landscape was so different from the desert where he grew up, Adam wasn't entirely sure if the strategies he knew would work here. Their jerky had stayed dry so far, wrapped in layers of salted banana leaf and buried in as much sea salt as they could harvest off the tarp, but the weather here was humid. It would surely go rancid before they finished it. He wished he knew how fast coconuts grew. He wished he knew if monsoon season would come upon them and change the entire equation.

Kalina leaned close enough to him that the ends of her hair brushed his skin, and he wished the moment would never end.

His desire for her hadn't abated, but had settled in for keeps, a soft, ever-present ache he could pretend was the same as missing pillows or ice cream or clean clothes, even though it was absolutely nothing like that. Other times he told himself it was human contact only that he longed for—the touch of another person as a basic life need. But he couldn't risk touching her, or he knew he'd never stop.

"Come on," he said at last and turned to head back to the beach. "I think we're having goat jerky for breakfast."

She laughed at that, a soft, musical trill like a tasting spoon of something sweet. It was not enough—not nearly, but he savored it anyway, smiling to himself and already picturing how to make her do it again.

That was the moment the world exploded. Fire burst through the arch of his foot and seared up his leg. His muscles seized and he stumbled in the surf.

"Are you okay?" Kalina was at his side, her hands on his skin, but he barely noticed. Gut-wrenching pain was traveling up his leg and over his thigh.

I stepped on a rock, he tried to say, but his tongue seemed to swell in his mouth, and anyway, he already

121

knew that couldn't be the truth, no more than anything else he'd told her that day. This was what was true: he was dying. He was going to die, right here on the beach, and Kalina would be left alone.

The palms of his hands didn't hurt. That was all that was left. He felt the sand, gritty beneath his fingertips, and knew no more.

~

There was a soft red glow all around him, like sunlight through your own eyelids, but Adam was sure it was fire. He was roasting alive. He was in hell, like his parents always said he'd be.

Opening his eyes felt like wrenching apart a coconut shell, and he couldn't see anything anyway. There were red shapes and black shadows in this corner of hell, and when one flitted closer, he cowered.

But no, it was only a child, a sweet, chubby child, with tawny hair like an upturned bowl on his head.

"Joshua," he choked. "Why are you here?" His little brother shouldn't be in hell. He was an innocent child, who'd never sinned a day in his life. Not like Adam, who'd run away and broken every rule his parents ever set, and died in a godless wilderness on the other side of the world.

Maybe this was a special South Pacific hell, fitted with pagan demons and inhabited by the souls of those lost at sea. But then what was Joshua doing here?

The little boy drifted closer, and looked at Adam with a pouty frown, his lower lip shoved out in that way he had. "I've been waiting for you, Adam. It's lonely here."

"I know, buddy. I know." He reached out his hand, but Joshua pulled away.

Demons surrounded them, their faces like the faces of sharks or pirates, their teeth as long as hunting knives. They held Adam against the ground and gnawed on his legs. He couldn't help it; he screamed in agony, and the demons grinned and kept eating, but no matter how much they tore at his flesh, there was always more, more, more. It never ended.

"Help me," he begged no one in particular.

"Shh," said a voice like the night wind, low and breathtaking in his ear. "I'm trying."

Warmth flowed across his leg, washing the demons away.

"Let me get another coconut shell." He knew that soft, lovely voice...from somewhere.

"She's so pretty," Joshua said. "Are you going to marry her?"

Kalina. There she was, fuzzy, on the edge of his vision, her dark hair like a mourning cloak. "No," he said, and was surprised by the weight of the sadness that came over him at that realization. "I can't. I'm dead."

"You should. You love her."

He couldn't explain it to a child, the difference between love and what he felt for Kalina. He didn't know what it was. Lust, certainly. And responsibility. And... requirement, sometimes, as if being without her would crack him in two. But it was too late for any of that. He was always too little, too late.

"I'm so sorry, Joshua. I'm so sorry I couldn't help you."

"Shh, Adam, rest. Stay still. Joshua is gone." That was Kalina's voice, and something cool was pressed against his forehead, and draped around the back of his neck. He turned in the direction of the sound, and Joshua loomed up before him again, his face pale, his eyes as sunken and bruised as they'd been those last weeks.

"Are you coming?" He looked so worried. So small.

"Yes," he groaned. "Wait for me, Joshua. I'll be there."

"No, you won't!" Kalina again, pressure on his jaw. "Stop that. You aren't going anywhere. Shit, Adam, this fever…" A horrid rattling sound, right by his ear. "You swallow this."

Some devil was shoving hot pokers down his throat. He gagged.

"No! Dammit, Adam…" The devil pried his mouth open again. "Good going. It's all sandy now. Just…"

There it was again. He was being violated by a demon, who was pouring gritty brimstone into his mouth. He tried to move, but the creature held his mouth shut and strangled him.

"I used to have to do this to our dog," Kalina growled now, half monster, half woman. "Don't mess with me, mister. And don't you dare fucking die."

Too late, he wanted to tell her. *I'm sorry,* he wanted to say. But he couldn't speak anymore. It hurt too much, the fire in his throat had become an inferno, the pain in his flesh a living, throbbing thing. And maybe Joshua was right, and he did love her, but what did it matter? Love wasn't strong enough to keep people from dying. That, Adam knew well.

"You aren't coming," Joshua said sadly. He was fading now. "You're going to leave me alone again."

"No," Adam promised. "No, Joshua. You don't belong in hell."

"I understand," the boy said, receding into the red and black darkness. "You're already in heaven."

fifteen

KALINA KNEW SHE NEEDED TO SLEEP. It did no good, to stare at Adam's foot in unadulterated terror for hours at a time. And yet, what else could she do? The thing was enormous — easily two times the size a foot should be, and an angry red at the source of the wound. Whatever he'd done to it was not something that could be fixed with the tiny tube of antibiotic ointment that came in Adam's First Aid kit. And she'd just given him the last dose of fever-reducer they possessed. Either his fever went down on its own, or he died.

He'd better not die. But even if he lived, what would they do if they had to amputate his foot? She'd already reached the limits of her medical knowledge. In the day and a half since he'd first passed out in the surf, Kalina had done things that even the indignity of butchering a goat hadn't prepared her for. There were days on this island that she'd wondered if there was anything left of Kalina St. Claire. After this, she knew the old her was well and truly gone, because if Adam only had the heiress to help him, he'd surely be dead already.

Hoping the injury was some sort of horrible jellyfish sting, she'd actually tried peeing on his leg, a remedy she and her friends had heard of and made fun of back on the yacht. She was so glad he was passed out for that. However, it didn't do anything to stop the pain, which meant it wasn't a jellyfish.

And that's what Kalina was afraid of. Jellyfish stings hurt like hell, but they were short-lived and non-fatal. By the time she managed to drag Adam up the beach and into their tent, he was writhing and incoherent, passing in and out of consciousness, and his foot had started to swell. There was a cut there on the bottom of his foot, and some sort of barb inside that Kalina had been able to pry out with the tip of a knife while Adam screamed in agony.

In all honestly, she didn't think it was the knife that was hurting him. She didn't know much about Pacific sea life, but she wasn't an idiot. There were poisonous creatures out there—stingrays and cone snails, lionfish and all kinds of nasty, deadly things. Kalina wished she remembered what that blonde boy had done for Brooke Shields in *The Blue Lagoon*. She'd stepped on some kind of poisonous animal too.

But Brooke Shields had still been beautiful, dying. Adam was as pale as the sand, and had vomited five times. There was nothing but bile left in his stomach now, and his skin was alternately cold and clammy and raging with fever. Chalk this up to one more reality that was nothing like the movies.

Kalina had rigged up a sort of waterproof sack from a piece of the tarp, and tried soaking his foot in cold water from the spring to bring down the swelling, but it didn't help. Later, she warmed water inside old coconut shells near the fire and singed every single one of her fingertips trying to pour hot water over his wound. This seemed to soothe the pain a bit, but it was hard to keep water warm in any large quantity. Coconut shells were all they had, after she accidentally melted one of their canteens, she didn't want to risk shattering the old vodka bottle.

By the first night, the fever dreams had set in. The one where he swore he was in hell with his little brother Joshua had been the worst so far. He'd screamed about demons and fought her as she'd tried to make him drink water and take medicine. Long after the Tylenol kicked in and he'd fallen into a restive sleep, Kalina had sat in the other corner of the tent, knees drawn up to her chest, rocking and wiping tears from her face so she could watch him twitch and moan through the darkness.

What if Adam died?

The next day was quieter, but no less scary. He flinched and moaned if she touched him, and wrenched up his face in pain if she lifted the flap of the tent to let light in. She tried to make him drink, but he threw everything up. And then there was his foot.

Sweet Jesus, save his foot. There was no reason for God to answer any of Kalina's prayers, but maybe He'd step in for Adam. Judging by the things Adam had said, they were on pretty good terms. Or used to be, anyway.

At some point in the afternoon, she'd nodded off, sitting up, cradling his head in her lap. She'd taken to periodically ordering him not to die. Bizarrely, he seemed to be listening.

When she woke, seconds or minutes or even hours later, he was staring up at her, and his eyes looked like the calm before a storm.

"Kalina." His voice was a croak, and his hand, reaching up to cup her cheek, was dry and hot against her skin. "I'm not supposed to touch you."

A tiny sound, halfway between a sob and a laugh, escaped her lips. "You can do whatever you want to me, Adam, as long as you don't die."

"Don't say that." His mouth twisted into a frown. "You are not a prize."

"Shh." She smoothed her hand over his brow, wiping the furrows away. "Rest."

"That's what he thought of you," Adam mumbled. His eyes were drifting closed again. "Bran. You were something he could keep on a shelf and show off. You had a tag with a dollar sign you carried everywhere you went."

"Hush, Adam…" If his last words to her were about what a shallow, petty bitch she'd always been, she'd die too. Of embarrassment.

"But he didn't know you. No one knows you."

She squeezed her eyes shut. Yes, that was true. And now no one ever would. She was going to die, alone, dead sober, on this island in the middle of nowhere. She was going to be a factoid at a cocktail party. That heiress who was lost at sea. Move over Amelia Earhart. Step aside, Patty Hearst.

"But I do."

Her eyes flew open and she looked down at him. The expression on his face was gentle, but his eyes said more. They always said more. They'd done so on the yacht, and on the lifeboat, and in dozens of random moments in the weeks since they'd been on the island.

She nodded, wordless, and bent her head over his face. Her hair fell like a dark curtain around them, shutting out his wound and the dim, messy tent. "Please don't die, Adam."

"I never touched you." His hand floated between them. "I should have touched you."

She pressed his hand to her cheek. "It's okay. Touch me now." She leaned in and kissed his palm.

Adam took a deep, shuddering breath.

"Are you okay?" she whispered into his hand.

"Don't stop." It was hardly a sound, but it echoed inside her like thunder.

Kalina smiled. "As you wish." She kissed his palm again, and the inside of his wrist, where his pulse fluttered far too fast. She kissed his forehead and each heated temple. Adam didn't move, but the creases in his brow melted away and the tightness in his jaw seemed to vanish. She dropped tiny kisses along that jawline, and then she reached his mouth.

Their lips met, the contact imperfect and upside-down, but the world shattered anyway.

This. This was the kiss that she'd been waiting her whole life for, the one she'd been born to give. And that's what it was: a gift. Not a prize or a reward or an item of bragging rights to take around and show to friends or gossip columnists. There was no one else in the world except Kalina and Adam, and their entire universe was nothing but this kiss. It didn't matter that his lips were dry and chapped, and his skin was still flush with fever. This was the kiss where vassals made oaths and princesses broke spells and brides and grooms became husbands and wives. This was the only kiss that ever was.

And when his lips grew slack against hers, and his head went heavy in her hands, she pulled away, and looked down at his peaceful face, and swept his hair off his brow.

"I will die happy now," he murmured.

"No," she insisted. "You will not die."

Not when she'd finally found him.

~

The next morning, two full days after Adam had first been injured, he was finally able to sit up on his own. His foot was still swollen, but the fever seemed to have broken. Kalina helped him hobble out onto the beach, and turned her face politely as he took a piss into the sand.

"I'm sorry," he said, as she helped him back inside.

"Don't worry about it." She bustled about, cleaning up the detritus she'd allowed to accumulate in the tent in the past few days— coconut shells and empty canteens, leaves and peels and dirty sand. They were beyond awkwardness about bodily functions now, right? They'd built latrines and butchered goats together. She'd held him as he vomited, which, she might add, was more than he'd done for her when they were still stuck on the lifeboat.

Of course, cocaine hangovers were a bit different than venomous fish poisonings, but Kalina was actually impressed with herself by how non-grossed out she was by it all. Back home, she'd always left the room when nurses would come to change her grandfather's various bags and tubing, gagging a bit at the indignity of the process. But here, it was just another fact of their existence, a chore that had to be done to keep them alive and functioning, no more embarrassing or inappropriate than getting food or water.

When she was done straightening up, she came over to examine his foot. It was tough to tell about the swelling. It didn't look quite as bad as yesterday, but it was still a mess compared to his other foot. "How does it feel?"

"Like goat meat," he admitted. "What happened? Did I get bit by a snake?"

"Stung by some kind of sea creature," she replied.

He frowned. "Probably a stone fish. Or a cone snail. Maybe an anemone. Did you see it?"

Of course Adam would know these things. Where had he been when she'd been freaking out the last few days? "No, Adam. I was too busy trying to make sure you didn't drown. I think you went into shock or something. I have no idea what it was."

He nodded, slowly. "Right. Sorry."

"It's not your fault," she said. "I'm just glad you're actually lucid. You've said some pretty crazy things these past few days." She turned to pull out some goat meat. He needed to eat something, and then back to bed. Maybe they should rig up some way to elevate his foot. That would help the swelling, right? Kalina began brainstorming ways to make a stand out of palm fronds and goat bones.

"Yeah. About that," he said, and something in his tone made her stiffen. "I apologize. I never should have said those things to you."

She unwrapped the meat from the banana leaf, and brushed off the excess salt. "What do you mean?"

"Just… forget it ever happened, okay? I feel terrible."

Her eyes burned, but she forced her expression into one of placidity as she turned to face him, goat jerky in hand. She didn't want to forget it. And she felt like she could fly.

"Here," she blurted, shoving the jerky at him. "Eat this."

Their fingers touched and her heart soared and she practically dropped the meat in his lap.

He looked at the meat for a long moment. "Kalina." He was begging. "Please. Don't make this awkward. I was delirious. I had no idea what I was saying."

"You seem to remember it fine." Was she *crying*? What a simpering idiot. What a silly little girl. She brushed the back of her hand over her face, smearing salt into her eyes, which only made them water more.

Adam was still looking down, as if there was nothing in the world more fascinating than goat jerky. "You know we can't," he mumbled to the meat. "It's not—"

"Not what?" she pressed. She couldn't help it. He was breaking her heart. It was shattered like the bits of coconut shells all over the floor of the tent. Not good? Not perfect? Not the only kiss that ever mattered in the history of the world?

He raised his head, and his eyes were dry, a stupid storm that never seemed to break. "It's not like that for us."

"Fine," she said automatically, armor snapping into place. "I don't care. I was just trying to keep you alive." That sounded moronic, even to her ears. Kisses don't keep people alive outside of fairy tales, and a fairy tale this was not. Adam didn't even believe in fairy tale things like true love. And she was dumb to imagine she did.

Adam said nothing, and after another moment, he started in on his jerky. She stood there, lost, for another minute, then gathered up all their empty bottles and stuck them in Adam's pack. She placed the final canteen near his thigh.

"I'm going to go get some water." She kept her eyes averted from his face. "And maybe some fruit. Don't wait up. You need your rest."

"Okay." He tore off another strip of jerky.

What had she expected him to say? *No, don't go? Wait, I was wrong? Kalina, thank you for saving my life, I love you like the sun?* It was ridiculous. Never going to happen. She whipped back the flap of the tent and headed out, her heart pounding and her stomach in knots. She never should have said anything, just laughed it off from the second he spoke.

What, did you think I actually liked kissing you? Sick, feverish, bad breath, barely conscious… gross. That would have been better. Or pointing out that Kalina St. Claire was way out of some deckhand's league. Or pretending like the entire incident had never happened, that it was just part of Adam's delusional fever dreams.

Kalina had started running, sprinting across the sand to the very edge of the jungle. She paused, panting, her hand against the trunk of a stripped-bare palm. It was getting harder and harder to find coconuts lately. They'd need to go deeper into the jungle to look—correction: *she'd* need to go deeper into the jungle. Adam could hardly walk with his foot like that.

Maybe this was a good time to start looking. She needed to keep her distance from him, anyway, until the humiliation faded and she knew exactly how she was going to act.

It was just a kiss, Kalina. She'd kissed dozens of men. Hell, she'd slept with over twenty. There was no way a single, upside down kiss with Adam Truman could trump all that. It was ridiculous. It was impossible.

It was absolutely true.

sixteen

ADAM ATE TWO PIECES OF BEEF JERKY and drank half the water. He rooted around in their store of fruit for something sweet to help wash the taste of salt and bile out of his mouth. With some difficulty, he dragged himself out to the latrine and back, and brushed his teeth with a piece of coconut. He examined his foot, checking for signs of infection, and found none. He thought seriously about drowning himself in the ocean rather than facing Kalina again.

It had been the right thing to say. The *only* thing to say. They couldn't go on like that. He hadn't spent the last month avoiding her only to throw it all away the second he was delirious enough to beg her for a kiss.

But, oh, that *kiss*. The salt smell of her hair, the touch of her breath on his skin, the feel of her full lips on his hand, his face, his mouth. She'd kissed him as if she were made to do so, and what's more, as if he were made solely for the purpose of receiving her kiss. They were a perfect fit, the two of them, like Aristophanes claimed in *The Symposium*—two halves seeking their Platonic whole. Adam hadn't been lying in the moment when he said he could die happy. Though he burned to have all of her, that single kiss was enough to survive on, a tiny slice of heaven, a ray of peaceful light to help guide him out of hell.

No. No, it wasn't. That was exactly the kind of thinking that got them to this point. If he could philosophize that they were the most perfect lovers in the world, he could just as easily craft arguments that proved this was all an artificial construct in his brain.

So then do it, Adam told himself. Once upon a time, before he'd gone off to the South Pacific, he'd been quite a good philosophy student. He could craft arguments with the best of them.

Adam wasn't in danger anymore, and so they could stop acting like it was the end of days. Kalina had saved him, that much was obvious. He didn't remember everything about the past few days, but he remembered enough to know that however much he had suffered, she'd been there to witness it and help him through it. It was an intense experience, and it was only natural that she feel some kind of attachment to him after that. But that's all it was. It would fade with time, was probably already fading, and soon enough, he'd only have to feel embarrassed by his own weakness, his own inconvenient obsession and lust.

The specter of Joshua rose up in his memory. *You love her.*

No! It was easy to think you loved someone when your entire survival depended on them. That didn't make it right. If Adam and Kalina were back in the real world, they would be nothing to each other. They weren't soulmates, they were shipwreckmates. What they felt wasn't love, it was loneliness.

There. Decided, he lay back down in the tent and went to sleep. When he woke, it was to the orange light of evening. He drank the rest of his water, ate another piece of jerky, then limped outside the tent to see if Kalina was only avoiding coming inside for the night.

The beach, however, was empty. No one had stirred the fire, so Adam got to work, making sure the coals were properly banked and there was fuel to see them through the night. As he struggled to bring in more firewood without putting too much weight on his bad foot, Adam couldn't help but feel mildly irritated at Kalina. Okay, fine, so she was mad. He could accept that. He could even understand that she might need time alone. There'd been plenty of nights that Adam had walked the beach until dawn instead of lying restless a few feet away from her. If Kalina wanted to go off alone for a bit, she had every right. But she'd only left him with one canteen of water. As he lay back down on the tarp, he strained his ears for the sound of her return, but eventually, exhaustion and darkness took him.

Hours later, Adam awoke to insane thirst, and a gray morning sky that cast the beach and the jungle in drab, ominous shades.

And Kalina was still gone.

This wasn't like her. The second he thought it, some part of his brain wanted to scoff at the idea. This was exactly like Kalina St. Claire. Spoiled and selfish and throwing a temper tantrum, regardless of the very real harm it could cause others.

Except… that wasn't Kalina at all. Not *his* Kalina, who from the moment they'd landed on the island had been practical and diligent and caring and willing—even eager—to learn all it took to survive. Kalina who'd helped him stand so he could pee the other day, who'd held him while he threw up, who kissed him when he thought he was dying even though he was probably the most disgusting specimen of humanity she'd ever gotten close to. *His* Kalina would never abandon him.

His Kalina was gone.

Adam was back in the tent more quickly than he'd thought he could move on his leg. She'd taken the pack, but not the First Aid kit or the lifeboat's single line. He packed those, along with a few pieces of jerky, and strapped them to his body with strips of the tarp he sliced off with his hunting knife. Then he did the same with the canteen and the knife itself. His swollen foot barely went into his sneaker, so he passed on lacing it up, and he cut himself a crutch of sorts from one of the tree branches they were keeping for firewood. As prepared as he could be, he limped his way up the beach to the start of the jungle. The trees rose high and thick around him, buzzing with insects and birdsong. The canopy was thick, the forest was deep, and Kalina was lost somewhere inside.

He shouted her name into the depths. It became a refrain, a call, every minute or so as Adam made his slow, painful way through the underbrush.

"Kalina!"

With every step, fire stabbed up his leg. The day grew hot and his voice hoarse before he even reached the spring runoff. He drank straight from the rock, and struggled to fill his canteen from the trickle. In the past, they'd climbed up to the grotto to fetch water, but he doubted he'd be able to do it on his own.

"Kalina!"

What if she'd slipped on the rocks and hit her head? What if she was up there, drowned and dead and only a few yards away? He stood at the base of the cliff, feeling as useless as he had when he was a teen and he watched his brother slip away from him.

"Kalina!"

No answer. His throat was raw and as he hobbled over to what used to seem like an easily climbable slope, his foot screamed with pain. He looked up at the top of the hill, where he knew the grotto—and hopefully the answers—lay. One shaky breath, then another, as his body rebelled at the idea of enduring so much agony. Then he tucked the crutch through the tarp belt at his back, lifted his injured foot off the ground, and began to crawl up the cliff.

It was hard going, even with most of his weight on his hands and good foot. His illness had drained most of his strength, and a climb that would have only taken a few minutes last week now seemed to last hours, with every inch won at tremendous cost. He had to stop and rest several times on his way to the top. And the entire time, a litany played on a loop in his head.

Please don't be dead. Please don't be dead. Kalina, my God, I'll do anything if you aren't dead.

He saw it a hundred ways. Kalina floating face down in the grotto. Kalina bleeding out, alone and scared on the cliffs. Kalina with her neck broken, a limp rag doll on the rocks. For weeks and weeks, he'd done everything possible to keep them both alive in this place, and the one time he didn't protect her, she wound up dead.

Please don't be dead. Please don't be dead. Kalina, my God, I'll do anything if you aren't dead.

As he crested the top of the slope, he noticed two things immediately. First: the pack sat open on a ledge of rock. Second: Kalina was nowhere to be seen.

His heart in his throat, Adam crawled over to the ledge and peered down into the grotto. Crystalline waters met his eyes, clear and cool and completely devoid of Kalina.

His forehead hit the ground in a mix of relief and despair. She wasn't dead in the grotto, but she was still missing. Gathering his strength, he shouted again.

"Kalina!"

The water bottles in the pack were full. Wherever she'd gone, she obviously didn't think she'd be away too long. A new collection of disasters sprung fully formed from his imagination. Maybe there were more pirates, and they'd happened upon Kalina, alone and vulnerable. Maybe…

Adam forced himself to stop. Envisioning all the worst-case scenarios wasn't going to do him or Kalina any good right now. He wasn't sure that it ever did any good, but after years spent preparing every night for the possible end of the world, it was a tendency Adam found difficult to avoid. His brain led him down all kinds of horrific paths, as if thinking them up would somehow help them not come to pass.

It had been easy to believe such things as a child, where day by day, despite his father's dire warnings, it never did end up being the Apocalypse. It grew more difficult as he became older, and the dreadful outcomes Adam tried to prepare himself for ended up happening. Josh had been carried away by his illness; Adam's parents stopped speaking to him; his job on the *Palanquin* was a disaster; the pirates had killed all his friends; he and Kalina had almost died on a lifeboat...

Only they hadn't died. Instead they'd found this gorgeous, wild place, and he'd come to know a woman Adam suspected even Kalina wasn't aware existed. And though he'd prepared himself every day for the worst—a water-borne illness, slow starvation, perhaps a tsunami or a typhoon—they'd been doing pretty well. With Kalina's careful nursing, he was even going to survive whatever it was that had happened to his foot.

And he'd be damned if he was going to survive it alone.

Adam grabbed a bottle of water and drank, then took a long, deep breath. Climbing up the slope had drained him more than he thought possible. And he still had to get back down. He still had to find Kalina. He leaned back, resting for a moment. She had been here. And she'd left without her pack. But why?

In front of him, the rock face of the cliff rose another ten or so feet, studded with lichen and tufts of wild grass. From time to time, Adam and Kalina had seen the goats up there, precariously perched on outcroppings and grazing at death-defying angles.

He peered closer. About five feet up, one of the tufts had been shoved loose, the grass and the clod of dirt it had been growing in flopping over the side of the stone foothold. As Adam examined this section of the cliff face, he noticed more flattened bits of grass, and, in one spot, four even depressions in the mud, like tightly grasping fingertips.

Kalina had climbed the cliff.

"Of course she did. Damn her." He'd barely made it up the slope. After another long drink, and a few minutes' thought, he undid his hastily-assembled contraption of tarp string and First Aid Kit, shoved everything but the crutch into the backpack, and even slipped off his shoes, tying the laces together and hanging them around his neck. He slung the backpack over his shoulders, looked up at the cliff face, and promised himself he wouldn't let her down.

Inch by impossible inch, Adam began to climb. He took long, breathless breaks between every step, hugging the cliff and praying for relief. His muscles burned, and fatigue threatened every second to sweep him off the rock. His foot had gone beyond pain now—everything below his left knee was no longer his own flesh, but an alien thing attached to his body with red-hot screws.

But he kept climbing. These, he imagined, were the Cliffs of Insanity that Kalina so loved to tell him about, and he was the farm boy who would scale any height to get to the princess.

He would find her. He *had* to find her.

As soon as he got his shoulders above the crest of the cliff, Adam abandoned all pretense of form and scrambled for purchase on the dusty surface, dragging the rest of his body up by pure force of will. He lay there, prostrate, barely able to move his head, for long minutes.

The top of this rock was overgrown with some sort of jungle vine, which ran in tangled mats across the stone. About ten yards away stood a lone palm, and several coconuts peeked out from under the leaves.

Well, that explained why Kalina might have come up here. But where was she now? Pushing himself into a sitting position, he took a deep breath.

"Kalina!"

The call echoed around the rock, deep and lasting. It faded away, and Adam shook his head. Nothing. Again.

Then, so faint a breeze could have drowned it out, he heard her. "Adam?"

seventeen

HER VOICE WAS THE SWEETEST SOUND Adam had ever heard. It came again, and this time, she was still faint, but clearly screaming her head off.

"Adam! Oh, thank God. Adam! Help me!"

He looked around, searching for the source of the sound. "Kalina! Where are you?" There was nothing up here but vines and rocks.

"I fell through the vines. There's a hole… Adam! Be careful!"

He crawled over to the edge of the vines. Up close, he could see the way they'd recently been pulled from their moorings on the cliff, and even closer, he noticed that the top of this rock was not solid, as he'd first suspected, and there was a massive hole that had completely been covered with vines, most of which were now broken and torn away from the sides of the rock. On his belly, he peered down into the crevice.

"Kalina?"

"Adam!" The cry that floated up out of the darkness was a mix of hysteria and relief. "Oh God. Adam! I'm stuck. My foot. I'm stuck under a rock. Please help me."

Yes. He didn't care if he had to learn to fly. "I'm coming. How far down is it?"

"I don't know. Maybe a story? Two stories? Please, please, help me."

Adam wondered if stories for Kalina were the kind with soaring loft ceilings, but decided not to bother her with that. He tied their line to a rock, then slowly began to lower himself into the crevice, his movements more a controlled fall than anything else.

How would they climb back out? He had no idea. Maybe they'd both die in a hole in the ground. He'd figure it out later. He wasn't going to leave her alone.

The crevice went down at a steep diagonal for about twelve feet, then opened up into a cavern. To Adam's surprise, there was light down here, and the distant roar of rushing water. As his eyes adjusted to the gloom of the cave, he could see dark pools scattered about the rocks, and Kalina, a few feet beneath him, pressed up against a boulder in waist deep water. Her eyes were as wide as dinner plates and she reached out to him like she wanted to leap out of her skin.

"Adam!" she screamed wildly as his feet touched the surface. A second later, he reached her, kneeling at the edge of the pool. Her skin was cold and clammy and she clawed at his arms, burrowing her face into his chest.

"Oh, Adam! Oh, Adam. I thought I'd never see you again. I thought I'd die here, alone in this cave. Oh Adam Adam Adam Adam…"

His name in her mouth had lost all meaning as a word, was just a jumble of syllables, a sound of desperate yearning, a fervent prayer that Adam felt, for the first time in his life, had an answer.

"I'm here," he whispered into her hair. "Everything is going to be all right."

And just like that, Adam let go of all the worst possibilities. He had her. It was going to be all right.

"Are you hurt?"

"I'm not sure. It hurt a little when I fell, but now I'm mostly numb. I'm stuck," she sobbed. "I can't get leverage to pull my foot out."

"I've got you. I'll push and you concentrate on moving your foot so it doesn't get broken while I pull you out. Can you do that?"

She nodded, sniffling. "Yes. Oh, thank God. I thought maybe you'd died while I was gone. I'm sorry I left you there. I'm so sorry, Adam."

"Shh." He smoothed her hair off her face. She was trapped beneath a rock in a cave and *she* was apologizing? Unreal. "Let's do this."

With the final shred of his strength, he wrapped his arms around her chest, braced his feet against the boulder and pulled. Kalina screamed as she popped loose from between the rocks, but Adam couldn't be sure if it was from pain or desperation. He dragged her out of the pond, cold and dripping, and she collapsed on top of him, crying hysterically, his name tumbling from her lips in an endless loop.

Adam held her until her sobs subsided, the two of them splayed awkwardly against the cool rock. He was so exhausted he couldn't move even if he wanted to. And he never, ever wanted to.

"I'm here," he kept saying. "I'm right here."

She clutched his shirt in her fists and cried harder.

Adam wasn't sure how long it was until her sobs subsided, and she went limp in his arms. He lay there long after, until he began to worry that it wasn't just exhaustion, but maybe hypothermic shock. She'd been in a cavern pool for hours, maybe even a whole day. With difficulty, he sat up and shifted her over. She started awake, and reached for him. Poor girl. He imagined she'd been awake all night, forcing herself to stay conscious so she didn't drown.

"Let me light a fire. We have to warm you up." His own shirt was clammy and damp from where she'd been lying on it, or he would have offered it to her.

There was dead wood from the vines here and there on the floor of the cave and Adam limped around, gathering them into a small pile. He started the fire with his tinderbox, and when he turned around, Kalina was already naked, her knees drawn up modestly to cover her lower half, her arm held protectively across her breasts. She pushed her wet clothes toward the fire.

"Come closer." He beckoned. "We have to get you warm, too."

Her eyes were downcast, and she didn't move. Right. Of course. He deserved that. Adam turned his back and cleared his throat. "I think the emergency blanket is still in the First Aid kit." It was a paper-thin scrap of foil, but it would give her something to cover herself with.

"Only my butt is cold," she replied.

He pictured her skin glowing in the firelight, her hair drying into those wild kinks.

"And I don't care what you see."

He was instantly hard, and really glad he wasn't facing her. She didn't mean it like that though. She meant that they were beyond that. Because they were. They weren't lovers, they were survivors. He wasn't her boyfriend, he was her teammate.

Carefully, he lowered himself to the ground, favoring his bad leg, and scooted, backward, toward the fire. When he felt the heat on his back, he stopped. "How is your foot?"

"Bruised," she replied. He heard her shift on the rock, maybe to warm her other side. "I think it'll start swelling once I get some circulation going."

"Can you put weight on it?"

"I'm not in a hurry to try."

"I'm not in a hurry to move any time soon either," he admitted. "I brought us some food though, and water. We can stay as long as we like." He pushed the backpack over to her, and heard her rooting around inside. After a while, there was the sound of chewing, and the slosh of the water bottle.

"What's that sound?" she asked after a bit. "It's like a river. I kept thinking I was going to get drowned by a wave."

There was indeed a distant roar of water. "There could be an underground waterfall," he said. "The same spring that feeds the grotto could bubble up somewhere else." Looking out through the cavern, he could see a haze of light, as if it opened somewhere down the way. Maybe they wouldn't need to climb out the crevice after all, a possibility that made him want to weep with relief.

But he had no desire to explore it now. He had no desire to do anything but sit near the fire and imagine her naked and warm and wonderfully alive, a few feet away. His chest still tingled from where she'd held on to him, from where she'd lain against his body and cried out his name.

"Okay," she said after a moment, and there was annoyance in her tone. "Now it's starting to hurt."

"You're getting feeling back?" He nearly turned his head, then remembered at the last second.

"Unfortunately. It's all pins and needles. My whole leg."

"Try massaging it," he suggested.

She was quiet for a second. "Can you?"

The words hung in the air, heavy with the fullness of cave echoes. Adam forgot to breathe. "Yeah," he found himself saying. "Okay."

He turned and Kalina was sitting there, hair brushed in front of her breasts, her shirt draped across her hips despite what she'd said about not caring. Her skin shone golden in the firelight, and her eyes met his, clear and gorgeous and free from all artifice. She shifted her injured leg in his direction and he moved closer, folding his good leg up beneath him and nestling her foot in the crook of his knee.

"Do you give good foot massages?" she asked.

"You're about to find out." On the boat, the girls had always been after him to rub lotion on them — their feet, their backs, their bare breasts. He'd avoided being part of their games, but the truth was, he was an excellent masseur. One of his first girlfriends, freshman year, had worked at a massage parlor and taught him all kinds of fun tricks.

He touched the ball of her foot and she hissed.

"Gentle!"

"Shh." He wiggled each of her toes, smoothing his thumbs across the ball of her foot until her face relaxed. "Let me do this."

He took his time, reveling in the chance to put his hands on her, in the freedom to warm her skin with his touch, to give her pleasure and relief, and to watch her expressions as he did it. He glanced down at his hands only rarely, keeping his focus on her careworn face. Her eyes were bloodshot, her face stained with tears, and she was the most gorgeous thing he had ever seen. Kalina stared back at him, her expression relaxed and unafraid, and just the tiniest bit curious as he moved to her instep, then her ankle, then her calf.

"Good?" he asked.

"Amazing," she moaned.

He glanced down, his fingers growing businesslike as they dug into her muscles. Her calves were still smooth, despite their weeks in the wilderness. She must wax or something. Adam's own beard was growing in patchy and pathetic. He'd never had much in the way of facial hair, unlike some of his brothers, who could go to full on mountain man in a matter of days. He probably looked ridiculous.

He cupped his palms around her calves and massaged the muscles with long, firm strokes, then moved up to her knee, gently bending and flexing her leg. She watched him, her eyes unreadable in the flickering light from the fire.

He moved up to her thigh. Her shirt was draped loosely across her lap, and when Adam lifted her leg to massage her thigh, his attention was drawn to the infuriating shadows the shirt cast at the apex of her legs. He could almost see, but not quite.

Eyes up, Truman. He raised his head to her face again—but no, that was a mistake too. Because there was no denying it. Her gaze was clear and steady and filled with intent, her mouth slightly parted, her lips plump and moist, as if she'd just licked them.

Slowly, his fingers crept across her thigh, until he reached the soft, fleshy area where any professional masseur would find it appropriate to stop. His hand froze.

"Don't stop," she told him.

He closed his eyes, as if it would change anything. She was still right here, still watching him, still practically in his lap and begging him to continue. When he opened his eyes, Kalina was all he saw. All he wanted in the world.

Adam nodded, once. "As you wish."

eighteen

KALINA WAITED AS ADAM'S FINGERS CREPT
HIGHER, into the crease of her thigh. She leaned
forward, her hair falling away from her breasts, and
pressed her mouth to his ear.

"Adam," she whispered.

He shuddered, and his knuckles brushed against
her clit.

"I spent the last day in this cave with my life
flashing before my yes. All the things I'd never be
able to do. Finish my education, get married, have
babies. All those milestones and moments."

"Haven't you been thinking about that since we
landed here?" His voice was rough, breathless, as his
fingers swept up against her clitoris, spreading her
wetness.

Had he? If they were back home, he'd be back in
school.

"But the thing that trumped them all was the idea
that I wouldn't see you again. That I would leave you

alone here. That I hadn't loved you when I had the chance." Her eyes fluttered closed in pleasure as the tip of his finger circled her clit.

"This is dangerous," he was saying to her, but he didn't stop. Two fingers now, pumping, rubbing, and she caught her breath and whimpered. He was going to make her come, already. He was going to make her come and he hadn't even kissed her. "Think about what you're asking."

"I'm asking you to take your clothes off." She grabbed the hem of his shirt and tugged. He stopped his activities for a moment and let her pull it off.

There. *There*. She's seen him shirtless before, in sunlight, starlight, moonlight, and just like now, with the firelight cutting deep shadows on his muscles, burnishing his skin like bronze. But this time it was for her. This time, she could place her hand on the planes of his chest, could run her fingers over the ridges of his stomach and tangle them in the line of hair leading down into his pants.

Adam was breathing heavy, trembling slightly under her touch. "If we do this, there's no going back," he told her, as if appealing to some sense of higher reason he thought would stop her.

But he was wrong. Kalina might be filled with desire, but she'd never been more clearheaded in her life.

"I don't want to go back," she said, undoing the button on his pants. She'd gotten glimpses of him naked before, of course, but she wanted all of him. She wanted to lay claim to his flesh, to lick his skin, to kiss every forbidden inch. "This isn't some survival instinct. This isn't lust or loneliness. I want because of you. Because of me. Because I'm a different person than I was before I got to this island, and I finally feel like I deserve to be with a man as wonderful as you."

Something came over his expression at that moment, like the sun breaking through the clouds, and whatever had been holding him back melted away. Adam cupped her face in his hands.

There was no pretense this time. No hesitation. He kissed her like he was possessing her, hard and long and breathtaking, his hands weaving into her hair. He kissed her with the combined need of weeks spent lying side by side, of wanting to touch so bad it burned.

Kalina clung to him, her fingers raking his shoulders as he eased her back against the ground, not breaking contact for an instant. He was her lifeline, and she was never letting go. His tongue was in her mouth, his breath short and ragged. She reached between them to get at the gaping fly of his pants.

Oh, God. There he was, in her hand, so thick and hard and hot enough to burn. As her fingers closed around his length, he broke their kiss, burying his head in her neck.

"Yes." It was a hushed, animal sound. "Kalina, my God, how I wanted…"

She stroked him and he seemed to lose the power of speech. With her free hand, she shoved his pants down his legs, running her palm up his sculpted thigh and over the ass she'd been admiring since they were back on the *Palanquin*. He flexed beneath her touch, thrusting into her hand, and she felt herself throbbing in response. For years, she'd been saying things like "I need you inside me" to her lovers, but now she realized what it meant. She *needed* him, now, more than breath or light or blood pumping through her veins.

"Kalina," he was panting against her skin. "We have to—"

"What?" she asked, maneuvering his pants down his ankles. As soon as he was naked he was all over her, pressing his body into the cave floor. This was going to kill her back. She couldn't wait. He was so hot, liquid bronze, covering her like a blanket. His lips caught hers, his hips settled between her thighs and she bucked up against him, rocking until he moaned into her mouth.

"Please," she begged him. "Please. Now."

But Adam held back. "I don't want to get you pregnant."

She smiled wide. "Oh, Jesus, Adam, is that all? Don't worry. I've got a thing. I can't get pregnant for at least five years."

The second the words left her lips, she thought of five years with Adam on this island. If they made it that far, would she want babies with him? And when he smiled down at her and kissed her as he rocked forward to enter her, she realized that for the first time in her life, she'd actually consider it.

But right now, all Kalina wanted was Adam, hard and thick—so much thicker than she'd expected—stretching her as he filled her to the hilt. He stopped then and rose up, searching her face for some sort of confirmation.

"Oh," she breathed, looking up at him with wide-eyed wonder. *Oh.* So this was what she'd been missing her whole life.

He grabbed his pants, balled them up and slid them beneath her hips, cushioning her body from the rock. "Are you okay?"

She lifted her legs and wrapped them around his hips, pulling him closer, deeper. "I've never been better."

"Kalina," he murmured against her lips. "You are so precious to me."

She traced his jaw with her hand, her heart too full of words to speak. *I love you, too.*

Adam began to move then, long, achingly slow thrusts where she could feel every inch of him, pressing and retreating. He studied her as he did, staring down into her eyes with such intensity, such intimacy that the old Kalina would have turned her head and looked away.

But now she stared right back, watched each micro-expression on his face as she clenched her muscles around him, watched each puff of breath as they crashed together, over and over, until a powerful tide rose within her, a rush of pleasure almost too perfect to bear.

"Adam…" she whispered, trembling, "I'm going to—"

"Yes." He drove into her, harder, faster, sweat forming on his temples from exertion or the effort to keep himself in check, Kalina couldn't tell. The muscles of his back bunched beneath her arms and his butt tightened under her calves. The fire glowed bright and golden, and when Kalina came, she was incandescent, as dazzling as the sun.

Over her, Adam groaned as his own orgasm hit and collapsed on top of her, cradling her face in his hands and pressing their foreheads together.

"Wow," Kalina managed.

"Wow," he agreed softly. "Are you okay? Do you need me to move?"

She held him tight. "No. No, don't ever move again."

He chuckled then, and slid out of her, but kept their bodies pressed together. "Never move? But there are so many things we haven't done." His hand slid down her chest to cup her breast.

"True. Well, I'll allow an exception for that."

"Good choice."

And as the night stretched out around them, they did just that.

~

Kalina woke to the sensation of Adam slowly stroking her back. His pants were back on, as were her shorts. At some time in the night, she'd pulled his shirt over her shoulders and rested her head in the hollow beneath his shoulder bone, and now she was surrounded by his mouthwatering scent. She pressed a kiss to his pectoral muscle.

"Hi," she said.

"Hi." A tiny squeeze. "How's your leg?"

"Sore. How's your foot?"

"Same. Do you need anything?"

She needed a change of clothes. A toothbrush. An enormous brunch with croissants and mimosas and French toast and ice cream. She needed a thousand more nights spent in Adam's arms. A hundred thousand. A million. How many years was that? She would live that long, if it meant she could stay with him.

"I mean, other than a way out of here that doesn't involve the use of our legs?" he added.

Right. Reality. Reality and survival. There were no long, lingering mornings-after on the island. There were rocky cave floors and old injuries and dried goat meat. But there was also Adam.

It was a fair trade.

The fire had burned down to red-tinged embers, but the night had passed, for the strange, diffused light was coming in from the crack far above their heads as well as the distant corners of the cave.

"Give me a second to get myself together and we can check it out," she replied, looking up at him.

"Okay." There was a moment's hesitation, and then he leaned in and kissed her, a full, sweet, good-morning kiss on the mouth.

Kalina closed her eyes and relished every last, delicious second of it. This was how it would be now. This was how it would be for both of them.

They retreated to opposite corners of the cave and returned a minute or two later, each smiling shyly at the other. Kalina had put her shirt back on, and handed him his own back.

"Aww," he said. "I kind of like how you looked in it."

"I don't think I'd like how you'd look in mine." She limped toward him. Her leg hurt some, but it was more stiff than anything. He still hadn't done up the laces on his injured foot. "Quite a pair we make, huh? Matching injuries."

"Yeah, don't think I didn't notice how you arranged for that. Can't ever let anyone else be the center of attention, can you?"

She laughed and grabbed the backpack. "Well, I'm going to carry this. Are you ready to go?"

"Almost," he said, and held out his hand.

She put her hand in his.

"Now I am."

A thrill ran through Kalina. Now, after months of never touching, it was like Adam couldn't get enough. He rubbed his thumb over the skin on the back of her hand and squeezed her palm as together they limped across the cave toward the faint light and the sound of running water.

They turned a corner and the sound grew louder. Here, there was a small cascade, about eight feet tall, spilling out of the rock and down into a second, larger cavern. This one was huge, with vast, arching ceilings, giant rock formations like tabletops, and a crystal-clear stream cutting through the center. At the opposite end of the cave was an opening covered with a roaring sheet of mist and water, and beyond that... a slice of blue sky.

Adam and Kalina just stared for a moment.

"Do you remember this waterfall from the outside?" Kalina asked.

Adam shrugged. "We haven't really gone too deep into the jungle yet."

It took about twenty minutes for the two of them to maneuver down the first cascade and into the larger cavern.

"This is beautiful," Kalina said, once they were on the lower level, holding hands again. "Like something out of a movie."

"Very beautiful," Adam agreed. "We'll need to keep this place in mind for when the rainy season starts."

Right. Of course Adam would be thinking that far ahead. Adam always prepared, and he always expected the worst. They wouldn't be rescued by the rainy season. They wouldn't be rescued at all.

"Over there." He pointed. "That's where we should build a little shelter. And over there"—he gestured across the stream—"a smoke house. And we could dry fruit."

Kalina could almost see it. Hand in hand, they strolled across the floor of the cavern while Adam pointed out features she hadn't noticed and things they should keep in mind, for the future.

For the future.

She paused for a moment and turned to him. "Adam, are you actually thinking this could work? *You*?"

He smiled sheepishly. "You're right. This cave could flood, or be difficult to access from the outside. I shouldn't make plans until we—"

Kalina silenced him with a kiss, rising up on her toes and throwing an arm around his neck. "Let's go see how accessible it is, you downer."

Together, they approached the waterfall. The ground here was slick and cool mist floated in the air. On the far left side, however, there was a break in the cascade big enough for a person. Kalina peeked through, then nearly slipped off the rock in shock.

The vista that met her eyes was spectacular. She stood at the center of a great, horseshoe-shaped formation in the cliffs. About ten feet below, the waterfall emptied out into a large, clear pool surrounded by a rim of rocks and cascading vines. It looked like something out of a travel magazine. A natural stair of boulders led down from the waterfall to the next level, and further into the deep jungle. The entire thing was lit with the rosy light of dawn as the brilliant sun broke over the trees and turned the waterfall into a sheet of diamonds.

"Adam," she called softy, in a voice she doubted he could hear over the roar of the water, "I think we made a mistake not exploring the jungle."

Adam joined her on the ledge, and whistled through his teeth.

"I dare you to say something bad about this," she teased, nudging him.

He stared down at the rocks. "This is going to be hell to get down."

Okay, he had her there. "We could always jump into the pool."

He shook his head. "Don't know how deep it is."

"Oh, Adam, don't you ever take chances?"

He turned and regarded her for a long, careful moment. Then he smiled, and jumped.

nineteen

THEY SPENT THE MORNING BY THE POOL, paddling around and lounging on the rocks. Kalina found a new tree bursting with ripe carambola, and they ate their fill, letting the sweet juice run down their chins and over their necks and then helping each other get clean again. As the sun rose high above them, they lay entwined on a bed of moss overlooking the pool, warmed by the rising heat of the day and each other's skin.

"This is paradise," Kalina murmured, tucked tightly to his side.

"You're kidding, right?" He stroked his hand down the curve of her spine. "We both, separately, almost died this week."

"Not that part," she said with a pout. "*This*. This is paradise. You, the waterfall, the fruit."

"No." He shook his head. "It would be paradise if we were on a little hike, and could get back on our boat at the end of the day and go back to civilization."

Kalina didn't look convinced. "I'm not sure civilization is all it's cracked up to be. I spent my whole life in the best city in the world, and I hated it there. I hated myself there. When I wake up on this island, it feels like I'm alive. Every dawn is the world born new."

He sat up then, considering this. "I suppose that makes sense, for you."

"It makes sense for everyone," she insisted.

"Not for me," he replied. "I was kept from civilization for my whole life. There was a world out there I wasn't allowed to be a part of, to even learn about. My parents rejected civilization, and all their children paid the price. Our education was warped, our understanding of the world was compromised. My brother even died. Turning your back on the world is no answer to dealing with its ills."

Kalina was silent for a long moment. "You're right. You were warped by having the world withheld from you, and I was warped by getting too much, too soon." She looked down at her hands. "But I still can't help but feel like this island...there's something special about it."

He opened his mouth to point out that, since they were stuck there, they might as well think it was a good place. But that was the old him, the Adam that was always waiting for a disaster. "It is special," he agreed at last. "It's special because this is where I met you."

That seemed to please her, and she kissed him, and Adam was glad he hadn't complained. It was wasted energy. They needed to heal, and find their way back home, and decide if they should move their camp inland, or to another side of the island, or up into this cave.

But not just yet. Right now, he wanted things that were much more simple. What he wanted to do was lick every inch of Kalina's body until she screamed into the treetops.

He deepened their kiss, pressing a hand against the center of her chest until she lay back before him, a delicious feast, damp and shimmering in the tropical sun.

"Again?" She laughed.

"Always," he replied. "You think this is paradise. Let's see how perfect we can make it."

She tasted of salt and starfruit and spring water, and he ran his tongue along the undersides of her breasts, loving the way it made her shiver, before latching on to one nipple while rolling the other in his fingers.

"Adam," she gasped, and wove her fingers into his hair.

He smiled, and nipped at the tight, brown nub, then nuzzled his way across her navel and to the thatch of hair at the cleft of her thighs. "I love how you say my name."

"How…"—another sharp intake of air—"do I say it?"

Like you love me. He rubbed his stubbly chin against her inner thighs and she squirmed beneath him, spreading her legs wide as he closed his mouth over her folds, teasing her opening with his tongue before circling it around her clit, then sucking, hard.

"Adam!" Kalina pulled his hair.

He smiled against her. "Again," he rumbled, and went back to work.

"Adam," she cried as he licked her, harder and faster, holding her in place with his hands as she bucked her hips ad writhed beneath his ministrations.

"Yes," he hissed and he could feel her flesh trembling beneath the vibrations of his voice. "Again." His dick was so hard, as if all these sexless months were finally catching up to him. He wasn't sure if he could even wait until she came. It didn't matter that they'd had sex twice last night, and again already this morning. He needed her, *needed*.

If this was Paradise, Kalina was a greater temptation than the apple.

Her fingers raked his shoulder blades. "Adam, Adam, please, I need—"

He was up on her in a second, flipping her over and pulling her up to her knees.

"There," he growled in her ear as he plunged inside her from behind. "Is that what you need?"

She shoved her hips back into him, groaning. "Yes."

He thrust, hard, one arm around her waist, the other palming her breast. *Mine*, he thought, and didn't even care. They were on the island. He could act a little wild.

And Kalina seemed to love it, anyway. She was there already, her muscles clenching around him, her breath coming in ragged, keening rasps, the sound hitting him deep in some forgotten, primal place he'd tried so long to ignore.

It was like this every time with her. She made him into a savage thing, a fierce and ravenous lover who yearned to possess every inch, who thrilled to the desperate, frenzied sounds that only Adam could make her make. His movements against her were fast, rough, and she shuddered underneath his hands, crying out as she came.

"*Mine.*" It was out before he could stop himself, as he thrust inside her once more, so deep, so deep, and waves of pleasure overcame his senses. The both slumped forward into the moss, Adam still buried inside her, his arms around her tight. Oh, God, what had he said? He couldn't speak, he was breathing too hard.

But his sweet, perfect Kalina merely arched her neck to kiss his jaw. "Yes," she whispered. "Always."

~

September passed, and then October. When November came, they started debating whether they should have crabs for Thanksgiving, or maybe lay a trap for some sort of tropical bird. Their store of goat meat was running low, and Adam was closely watching the remainder of the herd, trying to figure out the best strategy for maintaining the population so they could ensure a steady supply of meat. He'd shown Kalina how to tan the hide of the goat, and they'd made her a pair of what Kalina insisted on proclaiming "foot coverings." She'd refused to call anything so ugly "shoes." Adam didn't care, so long as she tied the damn things on so he could stop worrying that she'd impale her foot on a rock every time she stepped out of the tent.

It was raining regularly now in the afternoons, heavy downpours that would sometimes flood or even collapse their tent. Adam made regular visits to the waterfall cave, carrying up supplies and checking to see that the changing seasons weren't flooding out their safe space. If they needed long-term shelter, the cave was their sturdiest option, as long as the underground stream didn't rise during the wet season. So far, so good. If things kept up, they'd be ready to move into the cavern by the end of the month.

Adam looked forward to Kalina's plans for a Christmas palm tree.

That day, Kalina was off on a foraging trip. After the accident, it had been weeks until she'd been willing to enter the jungle without him, and even now, she never left without telling him exactly where she was going.

For his part, Adam was very careful about watching his feet any time he got near the shore. They'd made it through two whole months without any major brushes with death. Maybe they should make a sign: *Seventy-three Days Without a Workplace Accident.*

And what a fine seventy-three days it had been, too. Even Adam's pessimistic eye found little to complain about over the past few months. Okay, maybe he was sick of coconuts and goat jerky, but if the tradeoff was Kalina, it was a sacrifice he'd gladly make. On one hand, becoming lovers had changed everything for them, but on the other, Adam was constantly taken aback with how little had truly altered. They didn't need each other any more than they had before, and certainly didn't argue or tease less. Rather, he found it difficult to remember that they hadn't always been together, hadn't spent every night wrapped tightly in each other's arms, a cocoon of warmth and safety in a dark and wild world. He loved the way she kissed him; never offhand, even if it was a quick peck on the cheek in the morning, or a brush of her lips across a patch of bare skin. Kalina's kisses were always careful and sincere. Her mouth was a promise, and he was more than happy to meet it.

Adam was dragging driftwood up the beach when he saw the smudge on the horizon. For a second he thought the afternoon storms were coming early, but it was much too small to be a real storm cloud. He peered closer. It's a shadow, he told himself. It's nothing. It's impossible.

It wasn't. It was a boat.

He sprinted to the tent to grab his tinderbox, then raced down the beach to their signal bonfire. His fingers were shaking so badly it took half a dozen strikes of his flint to catch. He lifted the palm fronds they'd stashed nearby to fan the flames.

Come closer. Come closer. What if they were already moving away? What if they were too far to see the fire in the middle of the day? The fat-soaked wood was sending up black smoke, gorgeous, rancid smelling clouds, into the clear blue sky.

See us, see us, see us, see us, see us.

Minutes passed, and Adam could no longer tell which way the boat was facing, or if it was moving toward them or away.

No. No no no no no no. This was the first ship they'd seen since they got here. He knew the possibility of a ship passing by was so rare, he hadn't even bothered to calculate the slim chances of them seeing one, or vice versa.

They were going to leave. *No. No!*

In the air above the ship, a white flare popped and sparkled.

Adam whooped for joy. He jumped down off the rocks and ran back up the beach, waving his hands in the air.

"Kalina!" he shouted. Should he go get her? Or wait here? They saw him. *They saw him.*

They were saved.

If anyone was watching from the ship they must be concluding that he was a lunatic. He ran toward the jungle, then back down to the water, as if to make sure the boat was still there, the flare still glowing and smoking in the sky. He danced in the surf, did cartwheels, hollered at the sky. And the next time he turned inland, he saw Kalina standing at the edge of the forest, their pack slung over her shoulder, staring at him in disbelief.

"Kalina!" He ran at her, sweeping her up in his arms. "It's a boat! They've seen us. We're okay."

Her eyes were round and uncertain. "A boat? Are you sure it's not pirates?"

He laughed and swung her around in a circle. "That's my line. And no, I don't think pirates are interested in helping shipwreck victims."

Another half an hour passed, and the ship grew slightly larger in their sights. Finally, something flashed in the air above the boat, dark and metallic and gleaming like a bug. A helicopter. A few minutes later they heard it, the choppy, mechanical sound nearly alien to their ears. They stood on the edge of the beach, waiting, as the machine landed on the sand, tossing their tent flaps and the leaves of the palms under which they slept.

The helicopter door opened and a forty-something Middle-Eastern man in a smart, white suit stepped out, followed by two men in uniforms with guns.

Adam edged Kalina behind him. "Hello," he said. "Thank you so much for responding to our distress signal. My name is Adam Tru—"

"American?" the man asked.

"Yes."

"And the woman?"

Adam felt her hand on his shoulder as she peeked out.

The man's eyes widened, as did those of his companions.

"Wait," he said, and held up his hand in shock. "Are you Kalina St. Claire?" He pronounced her name like Sinclair.

Kalina nodded and took a few steps forward.

"Masha'Allah!" the man exclaimed. He turned to the guards and spoke rapidly in Arabic, then turned back. "You are very famous, Miss St. Claire. The heiress lost at sea. Have you been on this island all this time?"

"Yes," said Adam. "We both have. Since our ship was attacked by pirates."

"Believe me, habibi. The whole world has heard the story. I am Prince Amoud al Mohammed Edani, Miss St. Claire," he said. "And it would be an honor for me to take you home to New York, or wherever you wish to go."

"Thank you," Kalina said. "I think the nearest American consulate will do nicely, for me and for Adam. Right, Adam?" She slipped her hand into his.

It was then that Adam realized why she'd worded things that way. It had never even occurred to him that this prince fellow might only be interested in rescuing one of them.

The prince nodded. "Of course. How long will you need to gather your belongings? We will radio the ship to ensure guest quarters are prepared."

Adam and Kalina looked up the beach, at their faded red tent and their scattered belongings, the bits of rope and tarp and bottles and coconut shells that had seemed so valuable. Adam thought of how painstakingly he'd been carrying each of these items up to the waterfall cave, of how every one of them spelled the difference to them between life and death only an hour earlier.

"No," Kalina said abruptly. "Nothing here matters. We can go now."

twenty

FROM THE MOMENT THEY'D BOARDED the prince's yacht, things had been different. Even on the helicopter, Adam still had Kalina in his arms. She'd held tight to both of his hands and squeezed her eyes shut, pressing close to his side.

"What is wrong?" The prince asked Adam.

Adam shrugged, as if to say *none of your business.* "She doesn't like helicopters." Luckily, the sound of the blades kept them from having to discuss the issue further.

The prince's yacht was nicer even than the *Palanquin* had been. Adam watched as Kalina was shown to a stateroom that made even Bran's suite look pathetic — with a giant marble tub and more pots of soaps and creams and perfumes than one found in your average pharmacy.

"You going to be okay?" Kalina said as she turned back to look at him. "I really think I need a bath."

Looking back later, Adam would wonder if that was the beginning of the end. He'd wonder why he didn't question separate rooms. But Kalina seemed to find it perfectly normal.

Looking back later, he'd wonder about that, too.

The room the prince's servants had readied for Adam was only slightly less splendid than Kalina's, and Adam took his time bathing and changing into the simple but obviously high-end slacks and silk shirt one of the servants had laid out for him. When he looked in the mirror, he hardly recognized himself, his skin was so brown—darker even than it had ever been in the desert. And he was skinny— his jaw was sharp as a blade, his muscles stood out in stark relief. His hair was impossible—the servant offered to cut it for him, as well as shave his face, but Adam declined. He shaved himself, and put a bit of gel in his hair to sweep it off his face.

As soon as he was ready, he went looking for Kalina. There were nearly a dozen women wearing skimpy but expensive bikinis and swimming in one of the pools, but none were Kalina. After about twenty minutes of searching, he was directed to a sun-filled breakfast suite where Kalina and the prince sat at an ornate table groaning with food and wine.

He hardly recognized her, either. She was wearing red silk and eyeliner, and her wild hair was held back with clips made of gold. She looked like a queen dressed for court. She fit in well here, on the boat of an actual, real live Prince.

And, apparently, she'd gone straight for the baked goods and cheese. "Adam!" she'd called when she saw him approach. "You have to try these pastries."

The prince was sitting nearby, sipping something amber-colored and watching them in a way Adam did not find pleasing.

"We can't thank you enough, sir," he said, as he sat. "You have saved our lives."

The prince waved a dismissive hand in the air. "It is my honor," he said, "to assist in such a famous case."

Adam wondered if that meant he'd have been as honored if the shipwreck victims did not include an heiress like Kalina St. Claire.

"Prince Amoud," Kalina said, "Would you excuse us for a moment?"

"Of course," he said, and rose. "I will check on the progress of those arrangements you requested."

"Thank you."

When he was gone, Kalina turned to Adam with a smirk. "Sheiks, right? This place is crazy. Seriously, though, try the pastries." She shoved a plate at him, and a waft of burnt sugar hit his nostrils. Adam's stomach turned over.

"What is he talking about?" he asked. "What arrangements?"

She shrugged. "For when we land. Plus, giving him a job gets him off my back for a little while. Do you know he's already proposed twice?"

Proposed? Something hot flared behind Adam's eyeballs, which might have shocked him more than Kalina's news.

She laughed. "Don't worry about it. That's sheiks for you. They love wives. Amoud told me he already has, like, three. By the way, you clean up nice. Like the hair."

Adam's head began to hurt. "What arrangements?" he insisted.

Kalina rolled her painted eyes. "I'm making him take us back to civilization. I mean, this yacht is nice, but we need to get home. They're going to radio ahead and get in touch with my people so they know I'm not dead, and so it's not a total zoo with the press. That's all. Don't worry, Adam. I've got this handled."

Her people. The media. The multitudes who cared whether she lived or died. If Kalina was famous enough that everyone knew her story, did that mean that he was a part of it? What did "his people" think?

It was funny. For months on the island, Adam had been the one who knew what to do—how to light fires and butcher meat and set up tents. But he hadn't the foggiest clue how to prepare to return to civilization. Kalina seemed more than ready to handle it.

Later that night, he dressed for dinner, then headed to Kalina's room – locked. At the dining room, he found all manner of the prince's glamorous guests, but no Kalina.

"She's avoiding prying eyes," said one woman. "Can you blame her?"

"You fool. She's at a private dinner with the prince," said another.

Adam decided maybe he should take his dinner in his room. He stayed up until all hours that night, waiting for Kalina to come to his room, but she did not. The next morning he went to her stateroom to find her getting a massage and a pedicure from one of the servants.

"Where were you last night?"

She rolled her made-up eyes. "Didn't you get my message? When the prince who rescued you from a desert island asks for a private dinner, you say yes. It's just polite."

"Did he propose again?"

She laughed. "No, he asked for a private dinner to get my opinion on oil prices. Why, you jealous?"

Adam wasn't sure what he was.

"Don't worry, Adam, he's not my type."

Except what was her type? From the evidence, it was either assholes like Bran, or Adam when he was literally the only human in a five hundred mile radius.

"But at least that explains where *you* were last night," she said with a sly smile. "I waited up for you when I got back to my room. I don't even know which one of these cabins is yours. I thought you'd come find me. Wonder why you never got the message?"

Adam shrugged and kissed her glossy mouth. "No big deal."

And it shouldn't have been. They'd spent months with only each other for company. A few hours apart meant nothing at all. Right? And yet, even though they spent the day together, even though they passed that night in the same bed, even though he held Kalina in his arms, he couldn't stop thinking that when they got to the mainland, things would change.

But he still wasn't prepared.

After another full day on the Prince's opulent yacht, they reached land, where all of Kalina's "arrangements" came to fruition, as they were promptly whisked away in a dark-windowed town car and through a back entrance of a private clinic. They were separated for individual evaluation by medical

177

staff Adam swiftly gathered were Americans who had been hired for this express purpose. Kalina's "people" were clearly prepared. Adam gave blood and urine samples, and they examined the scar on his foot and set him up with an IV drip to "replenish nutrients." He was also given what one of the doctors termed "a mild sedative."

He was unconscious for at least twelve hours.

When he woke, he refused any more drugs and tore the IV from his arm. "Where's Kalina?" he barked at the sweet blonde nurse who'd been nothing but kind since his arrival.

"Sleeping," she said, and fluffed his pillow. "And you should be, too."

Adam couldn't sleep. He sat in the room, going slowly crazy. There wasn't much in the way of reading material. The Bible he had down. Travel magazines showing sunny tropical beaches and spreading palms held little interest for him. There was an old romance novel he read when he got really desperate, but the hero was a pirate, and it alternately disgusted him and made him think of Kalina's Man in Black.

"Sir, you should really rest," the nurse said the next time she checked up on him. But it was pointless. It was the whirring of the air conditioning in his room, the steady beeping of his medical monitors, the soft glow of fluorescent lighting.

It was the fact that Kalina was no longer at his side.

"I can get you a counselor."

He didn't want to talk to a stranger. He wanted Kalina. After another twelve hours, he figured she'd be up, and asked the nurse again.

"Um… let me see…" the nurse said, while checking his vitals. "I'm not sure about that…"

Adam was beginning to suspect his sweet, blonde nurse wasn't being entirely honest with him.

Half an hour later, she returned with a bland breakfast of toast and oatmeal and eggs. He hadn't seen food like that in months, and he realized now that he could probably live without it.

"Where's Kalina?" he asked as she put the tray on his lap.

"Eat up!" she said brightly. "The doctors say you need to put on at least ten pounds."

"I want to see Kalina."

"Please, Mr. Truman." She had kind eyes. "Please eat for me. I know you don't want another IV."

He shoved the tray off his lap and swung his legs over the side of the bed.

"What are you doing?" she cried.

"I'm going," he growled, gathering his hospital gown together in a bunch so he didn't flash the whole ward, "to find Kalina."

The linoleum was cold and slippery on his feet as he strode into the hall. The clinic was small, and the first few rooms he passed were dark and empty. Had Kalina's "people" rented out the entire place?

At the other end of the hall, he saw lights… and guards. One stepped in front of him as he approached.

"I'm sorry, sir, this is a private wing."

"I need to talk to Kalina St. Claire."

"There is no patient here by that name."

Bullshit. The guy was a wall in front of him. "Kalina!" he shouted.

A short man in a black suit entered the hall at this commotion. He put a hand on the guard's shoulder.

"Abel, Abel, I got this." He stepped forward hand outstretched. "Mr. Truman, so nice to finally have a chance to meet you. I'm Eric Norman. I'm one of Miss St. Claire's attorneys."

A lawyer? Adam shook his head. "Where is Kalina? Did you move her?"

Norman's expression was pained. "She's not accepting guests right now. She's been through quite a traumatic experience, as you know. She's got a lot to process."

"I'm not a guest," Adam ground out. "I need to see her."

"Right, well…" Norman looked Adam up and down. "Let's just go back to your room for now and chat. You're getting really worked up. I'll have the nurse bring in some Valium…"

"I'm not taking any of your drugs," he snapped.

Eric held up his hands defensively. "All right, tiger. Settle down. We're just trying to make sure you and Miss St. Claire recover. I can understand how stressful this has been for you. Escaping from pirates, fighting for your life on some godforsaken island…. But you can relax now. You're safe. Everything is going to be fine."

No, everything was not fine. And he wouldn't feel safe until he'd gotten to Kalina. "You can't keep me from her."

The short man straightened and gave him a withering look. "Buddy, we can do this the easy way or the hard way. Which do you want?"

Adam apparently wanted the hard way, but he was no match for two guards and an orderly with a tiny glass syringe. As blackness crowded the edges of his vision, he looked up into their strange, impassive faces.

"Please," he begged, though he knew it would do no good. This was the expression his father used to wear every time he beat his children. The dead-eyed, plastic one that meant you were doing something wrong and didn't care.

Kalina…

~

The next time Adam woke, it was to a bright and sunny hotel room, and a smiling Eric Norman sat at a table across from him, folding his hands over a large stack of papers.

"Good morning, Mr. Truman," he said with false friendliness. "I'm so glad we're getting this chance to chat."

Adam started up, which was when he saw the enormous guard by the door. Warily, he leaned back against the pillows.

"I do hope you feel rested now," Norman said. "The doctors tell me that it can take some time to recover from trauma like the one you experienced."

"The one where I was attacked and drugged?" he asked.

The lawyer chuckled. "Being trapped on a desert island. Now, let's see." He shuffled through a few of the papers in front of him. "We did attempt to contact your family and let them know you were all right, but no one has returned our letters, and there is no phone at their…farm." He made a face at the word, as if at a loss to describe the Truman's ranch.

Adam didn't dignify that with a response, or even much of an expression. Did the man think he was imparting new information? Trying to hurt his feelings? They probably hadn't even opened the letter mentioning his disappearance at sea, let alone one explaining that he'd been found.

"Is there anyone else we can contact for you?"

"Kalina," he said flatly. "Tell her I need to see her."

Norman gave him a lopsided smirk. "You're a one-track kind of guy, aren't you, Truman? Okay, then. Let's move on." He opened another folder. "Right, so…. your stay here, and all your medical needs, have come to a sum total of about twenty-four thousand dollars, give or take. Private nurses don't come cheap, my friend. It's a pity you chose to sleep through most of your sponge baths."

Adam felt the blood drain from his face. "How long have I been here?"

"Ten days." The man was examining another sheet of paper. "Of course, as Miss St. Claire's representative, I have no problem making sure you receive the best of care. She's been quite adamant on that point."

"Where is Kalina?"

Norman continued as if Adam hadn't said a thing. "We'd also like to extend that hospitality to your voyage home. First class plane tickets, a car at the airport to drive you back to…" he paused. "Will you be heading to New Mexico or to your campus in Maryland?"

He'd missed an entire semester of school. *Oh no. His scholarship…* "I don't know if I'm still enrolled."

The lawyer pursed his lips. "The semester, I'm afraid, is over, but your dean has been informed of the special circumstances surrounding your absence. If you are ready to return to academia in January, you will find that your space, and your funding, has been reserved."

Adam stared at him.

"See, Mr. Truman? I am not your enemy. I am only here to assist you. Miss St. Claire wants to ensure that you are able to return to your normal life as soon as possible."

His normal life? He didn't have a normal life. He was an orphan with an enormous family. He was a student who had disappeared from school. He was in love with a woman who'd posted guards outside her door to keep him away.

Why had she vanished the second they'd gotten to the mainland? Why had she sent this… this toad here to deal with him? And what did he mean about his funding?

"I can't imagine the difficulties you've been through, but from Miss St. Claire's accounts, it was quite wretched."

Adam fought to bring up a memory in his mind of Kalina swimming in the grotto or dancing in the dawn, of her dropping kisses on his chest and calling the island paradise. But that's not what he saw. He saw her lounging in red silk and gold jewelry on the yacht of a prince. He saw her turning and looking at their pathetic little tent one last time.

Nothing here matters. That's what she'd said.

"The last thing I want you to do is suffer any more from this ordeal," the lawyer was saying now. "The investigation regarding the violent takeover of the *Palanquin* is still outstanding, you know. Even though all the passengers and the captain were successfully ransomed, the Nesbits and their insurers are determined to see someone pay for these crimes. It's been quite difficult to keep the investigators away from you and Miss St. Claire."

"I'm happy to give a statement," Adam said.

Norman gave him a pitying look. "I must tell you, they find it very curious that you, alone among the crew, managed to survive." He pressed a hand to his smarmy lawyer chest. "I honestly can't imagine what they think they'll gain by interrogating you. But with Miss St. Claire unconscious for the entirety of the attack, they are certain that you know something about the pirates who stole their ship."

Adam swallowed. "I don't!"

"Of course not. And I am more than happy to continue representing you, and your version of events, to any and all curious parties. No one will bother you as long as you do as I say."

He went cold as he realized what the lawyer was saying. Tens of thousands of dollars for his medical care. Making sure his college funding was in place. Protecting him from the horrible Nesbits and their equally horrible theories. Of course. This was about money. Everything with people like this had to go back to money. A few months on a desert island and he'd completely forgotten.

It seemed Kalina hadn't.

"What do you want?" Adam asked.

Norman beamed. "What's best for you, of course. I want your life to go on as it was before. My understanding from discussions with your dean at St. John's was that you were one of the most promising students in your class. Do you have any idea how much your life can be derailed by media scrutiny? As you can imagine, this case has quite captured the public imagination. The heiress lost at sea! We haven't yet decided our entire media strategy, and I wanted to give you the opportunity to opt out now."

"Opt out?"

"Yes." Norman handed him a stapled set of papers, riddled with colored stickers next to blank lines pre-printed with his name. "The servant who survived with her is not really part of the narrative. You understand. Miss St. Claire is prepared to pay you quite handsomely, not only for everything you did to help her survive on the island, but also for respecting her privacy, both in terms of the media and regarding any future contact."

He wasn't part of the narrative? Of course not. The second Adam stopped being useful, there was no reason to pretend he even existed.

Adam scanned the sheet. "Fifty thousand dollars?"

"That is, of course, on top of covering all the aforementioned medical and travel bills. In addition, there is a new wardrobe waiting for you whenever you check out of the hospital. Miss St. Claire was adamant that you be taken care of."

Taken care of. Maybe he was lucky she hadn't chosen to have him bumped off, instead of merely paid to disappear from her life. Her *narrative.*

Nothing here matters. Their life on the island was a mirage, a stolen season, vanishing with a single pen stroke.

He should have known. After all, he'd been down this road before, when he'd gone away to college. Only he had never been paid for the privilege. If his own family could turn their back on him, why did he expect any better from Kalina St. Claire? No matter what had happened between them on the island, it wasn't built to last. There was no such thing as true love.

Adam signed the documents, his heart heavy in his chest.

"Good boy," said Norman, clapping him on the shoulder when he was done. "I promise you, this is for the best. You'll be so relieved to put this all behind you."

Adam could agree with that. He just wasn't sure what lay ahead.

twenty-one

"AND THAT IS HOW I LEARNED TO to skin a goat." Kalina squeezed her grandfather's limp hand. His skin was dry and papery, and there seemed to be nothing but bone beneath. She had no idea if he even heard her, let alone understood her. The doctors all said even when he was conscious now, he wasn't lucid anymore.

She'd missed her chance. Even though the family lawyer, Eric Norman, had hustled her out of the South Pacific and home because of her grandfather's failing condition, she hadn't been able to get to him in time to say a real goodbye. All she could do was sit here and talk to a vegetable.

So she did. Hour after hour, she told him about the months she'd spent on the island, about the things she'd learned with Adam.

"I'll bring him to see you too," she explained. As soon as he was well enough to travel. The poor man.

Eric had told her that when the doctor's had examined Adam, they'd found he'd picked up some kind of horrible parasite. At the time she'd left the clinic, he was on such heavy medication that he'd had to be sedated. Kalina had felt so guilty for leaving without talking to him, but Eric assured her that Adam would receive the best medical care possible, and Eric himself had stayed behind to make sure her wishes were carried out. Oh, Adam. He must have been in excruciating pain for who knows how long, and he'd never let on. That was just like him, though, wasn't it? Always so silent and stoic and brave. They'd have to have a serious conversation about it when he came home.

Home. She had no idea what that would even mean now.

Adam would want to return to school, of course. She'd also given Eric instructions to follow up on Adam's enrollment at college. He'd already missed a semester. Kalina wasn't sure how that would affect his scholarship, but that hardly mattered now, did it? What did college cost, anyway? Ten thousand? Twenty? The important thing would be figuring out logistics. Could she move to Annapolis while her grandfather was so ill? Would Adam be interested in transferring to a school in New York?

They'd cross that bridge when they came to it. The important part would be getting Adam healthy, and back where he belonged.

With her.

After another two days at her grandfather's bedside, she called Eric. "I want to speak to Adam. Hasn't he woken up yet?"

"Ah, kiddo, these things take a little time. He's not well, you know. It's been complicated."

"Well, can you have him moved back here?" Kalina didn't like the idea of Adam recovering half a world away, surrounded by strangers.

"The doctors say that's risky. Such a long trip. I think we're much better off if I get this all squared away before we get back to the U.S. You just lay low. You haven't been going out or anything, right?"

Kalina laughed. "Are you kidding?" Eric had her on a strict media blackout until he returned. She wasn't even allowed to contact her friends from the *Palanquin*. Something about a lawsuit with the yacht's insurers.

"Don't take that tone with me, young lady. You and I have been down this road before."

That was true. Eric had a ton of experience getting her out of media messes. He'd personally marched into nightclubs and extricated her coke-fueled ass from bar fights or paparazzi blowouts. Of course, she'd been a different girl then. Eric would see, soon enough.

Everyone would.

~

Kalina stared at Eric in shock. "What do you mean, he doesn't want to see me?"

Eric shrugged. "Don't shoot the messenger, kiddo."

"I want to talk to him."

"Kalina, come on. Be fair to the poor boy. I think he's made it pretty obvious he just wants to be left alone. Hasn't he given up enough of his life to see to your every need?"

Kalina winced. That wasn't what it was like. Adam wasn't her servant on the island. He was her partner. Her savior. Her lover — a fact which Eric had hand-waved away. But Adam wasn't like those other guys, who pursued her one second and vanished into thin air the next.

"This doesn't make sense," she said. "Is it because I left him at the clinic? You explained about my grandfather, right?"

"Yes, but, Kalina…" he pulled up a chair, sat down across from her, and cleared his throat. "Come on. You're not a child anymore. You have to think about this reasonably. You know who and what you are, and who and what he is. You're Kalina St Claire, the heiress who survived a desert island. This is great for you, great for the company, just great. Truman isn't part of that story."

"Yes, he is," she insisted. "He saved my life."

"Are you absolutely sure about that?"

"What?" She narrowed her eyes.

"Look, Kalina. I don't know what that boy was doing on the yacht that night. I'm not sure what either of you were doing — he should have been in his quarters, and you should have been with your boyfriend. But you weren't. You should be grateful Bran Nesbit's decided to keep that part of the story to himself."

Kalina should be grateful? Bran should be thanking his lucky stars she wasn't out telling the world he was a sadistic little dickhead.

"And the last thing we want is for the public to turn on you. Survivor heiress is great for us. Cheating slut who let her boyfriend be captured by pirates? Not a good look."

"Bran's not my boyfriend," she said. He hadn't so much as sent flowers, though she knew he knew she'd returned.

"And neither is Adam Truman," Eric pointed out.

No, *boyfriend* seemed a paltry word for what she and Adam had. Or used to have.

"I understand you've been through an intense experience. I'm not sure you can trust your feelings on this issue. Look at what a few weeks apart has done for Adam. He's trying to get back to his life. Maybe you should do the same."

"I don't care what you think!" she exclaimed.

"You seem a little anxious. Where are your pills?"

"I don't want them." She crossed her arms over her chest.

"The doctor said—"

Kalina tuned out. The doctor had said she was traumatized by her experiences and put her on massive doses of Valium. Kalina had flushed every pill down the toilet. She was done with drugs that gave her artificial feelings.

"—after something like what you went through. But you can't let it rule your life. Your grandfather wouldn't want that. Something terrible happened to you on that island, Kalina."

"Something wonderful happened to me there," she snapped. "I was reborn."

"Reborn?" The lawyer's eyes widened and he gave her a concerned look. "All right, kid. I do not pretend to understand what you're feeling right now.

You've been through hell and back. And there are a lot of people who are going to be more than willing to take advantage of that. It's my job—not to mention my duty to your grandfather—to make sure that doesn't happen. I've protected you from the Nesbits, I've protected you from the media, and now, I'm going to protect you from Adam Truman. He's gone, Kalina, and you are not, under any circumstances, going to go after him."

"Excuse me?" She shot out of her chair. "You can't tell me what to do!"

"I looked into his past, you know. He grew up in some backwoods cult, published all kinds of radical philosophy in his school's newsletters, and was making quite the habit of ingratiating himself with the rich and powerful. That kid is bad news."

"What do you think he's going to do, put me in his cult?" she asked, tossing her head. "You don't even know him."

"I know enough. You think he was some kind of miracle worker out there on the island, but I can promise you that one butchered goat doesn't count for a whole lot in the real world."

Kalina tucked her chin into her chest. "We butchered the goat together," she murmured.

Eric stared at her, incredulous. "Exactly. God, listen to yourself. This is a man who likes to butcher goats. Be lucky he didn't decide you looked tasty too."

"He *loves* me."

"Then where is he?" Eric spread his hands. "Gone, just like all the others. They are scumbags, Kalina. After whatever they can get from you, and when they realize they can't, they crawl back into the hole where they came from. Don't you see I'm just trying to protect you? He's the kind of guy who'd take serious advantage of you – of your entire family. It's my *job* to keep that from happening.

"Oh, yeah?" asked Kalina. She put her hands on her hips. "So it was your *job* to make sure Adam doesn't want to see me anymore?"

Eric said nothing.

Holy shit. Kalina thought about guys she dated, the ones who seemed to vanish overnight, before she'd started dating only fellow elites like Bran. She'd always thought they'd lost interest in her, but what if it was more than that? What if they'd been chased off by her family's pitbull lawyer?

"What did you do, Eric?"

He gave her a scathing glare, then strode across the room to her grandfather's desk. "I did my job. It's a standard contract. I use it all the time with the undesirables you like to drag home. Truman, I admit, got a little more in consideration of, well… everything. But he took the payoff, like all the rest." He pulled a sheaf of paper out of one of the drawers and slapped it on the surface.

She couldn't even look at it. "That is not your decision to make!"

"Please," he scoffed. I'm here to protect you. Don't you want to know they're only in it for the money?"

"You should talk!" she snapped. "You keep talking about how this is just your job. Would you be *protecting* me if we weren't paying you?"

"No, Kalina. That's what makes it a job. I don't pretend I'm in love with you. Sometimes acting like I like you is more than I can handle." He pointed at the stack, then headed for the door. "There. Read it and weep."

Kalina just stared at the pages as the door slammed shut behind her. Then she sat down at her grandfather's big, leather, chair, and opened the contract.

She read it. She wept.

~

Two days later, her grandfather fell into an intractable coma, and Kalina made the decision to stop life support. She stood in the private hospital room, watching the endless beep beep beep of the monitors.

"You're sure he doesn't feel anything?" she asked the attending physician.

"He's already gone," the doctor confirmed.

Kalina wasn't comforted. "Part of me feels like he's been gone for years. Once he couldn't talk to me, didn't recognize me—"

"He recognized you, Kalina," the doctor said. "His vitals were always better after you visited. Just because he didn't speak didn't mean he wasn't aware. If anything, I think he was hanging on these last few months in hopes that he'd see your safe return."

Kalina thought about all those years she'd avoided visiting, preferring to drown her troubles in drugs and alcohol rather than the silent confidence of the only man on Earth who loved her.

"How do you do it?" she whispered. "How do you take care of people who are dying?"

"I don't," said the doctor. "I take care of people."

194

It was, Kalina realized, that simple. How odd—she'd understood it well enough on the island. Adam hadn't been anything but a fellow human in need, and she'd met his needs to the best of her limited ability. Anything she could do to help him, she had done.

She looked around her grandfather's room, at the state of the art machines and medicines, and thought back to their tent, to her sandy fever reducers and pathetic coconut shells of warm water. All around the world, people were doing the best they could with whatever they had. Once, Kalina had been one of them. If she was brave enough, she could be one again.

Twelve hours later, Charles St. Claire was gone. Kalina had spent his final hours holding tight to his hand, and telling him about her dreams.

~

Kalina St. Claire's first act after signing the papers that turned over the bulk of the SC International to her was to fire Eric Norman. By the time the funeral was over, his firm had sent over the records from their tenure as the family's personal lawyers, which was when Kalina discovered the full extent of the man's meddling in her personal affairs.

Yes, he'd kept her out of trouble for many years – but he'd given her a fair share of it too. Not including Adam, he'd paid off nearly half a dozen lovers he'd deemed unfit for the family. He'd bribed photographers and journalists to keep unflattering stories about her out of the papers. He'd even paid off legal fees for her drug dealers to make sure they never delivered her name to the press. And she'd known nothing about any of it.

God, she'd been naïve.

Kalina had almost called Adam on the spot, but there was one thing that had been keeping her. Eric might have offered him a bribe, but Adam had been the one to accept it.

He'd rather have money than Kalina.

So maybe Eric was right and she should get on with her life, her plans, and forget what had happened on the island. After all, Adam could do it, and he only had a fraction of her money.

That approach worked for all of three months, then Kalina broke down and hired a private detective.

~

"No, I have the records that the check was deposited," Kalina said into the phone, tapping the edge of her pen against her grandfather's giant mahogany desk. She had a stack of reading to do tonight. But it could wait fifteen minutes.

All she had to do was find out how Adam was doing and then she could move on with her life. She'd know what he'd used his filthy payoff for, how much he was enjoying his disgusting earnings, how little he cared what had happened to her.

"Yes," said the private investigator. "But he doesn't have it anymore. He put the entire amount into a custodial account. There are twelve beneficiaries."

Twelve? Kalina felt cold. "All named Truman?"

"Yes. Do you need their first names?"

"No," she replied. She could name all twelve of Adam's brothers and sisters without the detective's help. Stupid Adam. Didn't he know that when he accepted bribes, he wasn't supposed to go out and get all noble with his misbegotten earnings? He certainly wasn't supposed to set up a trust fund for his siblings, in case they too wanted out from underneath their parents' control.

"So then how is he paying for school?"

"He seems to have two campus jobs. And he was able to retain his academic scholarship. But I wouldn't say he has it easy by any stretch of the imagination."

That made no sense. He was supposed to have it easy. He'd given her up so that he could have it easy. That's how payoffs *worked*.

Unless… he hadn't cared about the money.

"What else?" she asked now, as the hand holding her pen began to tremble. Eric had told her that Adam wanted money more than he wanted her. But what if the truth was even worse? What if he'd wanted neither of those things?

The private investigator went on. "His transcripts show no substantial difference from before and after his absence. His teachers describe him as equally dedicated and active in classroom discussions. He's on track to graduate on time despite missing a semester, and with highest honors."

Kalina started drawing on the pad, her pen making deep black gashes like scars across the page. "That's…wonderful." And it was. It was great to hear that Adam hadn't wasted any time getting back to the life he'd always intended on having. She remembered what he'd said on the island, about how much he missed civilization. The entire time she'd been

197

discovering herself, he'd been missing out on the person he always wanted to be—the one he'd given up his family and everyone he'd ever known to become. To her, the island was a paradise, dangers and goat meat and all. But to him, it was a prison.

The P.I. went on describing Adam's movements and classes and what she supposed passed for a decent social life at his Annapolis college campus. She wouldn't know—her pastimes before the shipwreck did not resemble his in any way, and since the island... well, she didn't have a social life anymore.

The angry marks on the legal pad began to cover all the yellow. Adam participated in trivia night at a campus pub. He attended guest lectures on Friday nights. He volunteered with a local literacy group, working with at-risk children.

He didn't seem like he missed her much at all.

What did they have in common, really? On the island, their differences hadn't been so noticeable. He wasn't a student, she wasn't a socialite. There were no clubs for her to party at while he spent his evenings reading an entire library.

And neither of them, if given the choice, would want to spend their lives drying goat meat and weaving palm frond mats. She hadn't butchered a single animal since returning to Manhattan.

Maybe, to Adam, Kalina was a goat. Good enough for the island, but not something you'd have if steak or lobster was on the menu.

Her pen tore through the page.

Adam was lobster. He was Kobe beef and foie gras and beluga caviar. There was nothing like him in the entire world.

"Dammit."

"Ma'am?"

Right, the investigator. "Is he dating?"

"No," he replied right away. "No romantic entanglements whatsoever."

Kalina took a deep, shuddering breath, then let it out. Thank goodness for small favors. She didn't know if she could bear the idea of Adam with another woman.

"Thank you for your work," she said.

"There is one more thing I think you should know," the detective added. "I had the opportunity to visit Mr. Truman's dorm room the other day, when he wasn't in."

"Yes?"

"That issue of *Time*? The one with you and your story on the cover?"

Kalina rolled her eyes. She'd refused to be interviewed for the article, and cringed at what the magazine had written about her and her time on the island. And the picture of her in a bikini, lounging on the deck of the *Palanquin* with a champagne flute in her hands. Kalina had seriously considered not going to class the entire week the issue was on stands. "What about it?"

"He keeps it in his bedside drawer."

Deep inside her, a microscopic spark of hope flared to life. *Don't be silly, Kalina.* He must have bought it because he wanted to see what it said about him. If it said anything at all. It was that simple.

But he kept it.

"I think I have everything I need for now. Please send along a final invoice." She hung up and dropped her head into her hands. Hiring the detective was supposed to be the end of all this. Just find out that

Adam was fine and happy, and move on with her life. Only now she was more conflicted than ever.

As far as she could tell, Adam hadn't felt any great moral quandary about accepting money to stay away from her. He hadn't even done it for the money. It appeared as if he'd been planning on letting their relationship wither anyway.

And yet, he wasn't dating anyone else. Still, that alone meant nothing. He was busy with school, work… maybe he didn't have time to date.

He'd kept her picture. Though that didn't necessarily mean that he missed her. That he loved her. Maybe it was nothing more than a keepsake of a time he was glad to put behind him.

Maybe if she kept telling herself that, she'd be able to get all these crazy ideas out of her head, get *Adam* out of there. Everything else Kalina had tried had been a failure—getting involved in the family business, going back to school, even breaking down and hiring a detective to give her some damn closure.

So why wasn't it working?

Nothing made a difference. Time, distance, contracts—she would never stop feeling this way. Kalina knew it. This was what she'd been searching for – like the movie said: this was true love, and it didn't happen every day.

With a deep breath, she faced the truth. She needed Adam like she needed the dawn, and she wouldn't stop until she got him back. It took Westley five years to find Buttercup. She could do better than that.

Only… how to get him back?

Kalina had been proposed to by sheiks and ogled on Page Six and desired for her beauty and her wealth her entire life, but she wasn't good enough for Adam Truman. Not nearly.

Not yet.

twenty-two

ADAM TRUMAN WALKED ALONE back to his dorm room, the edges of his black graduation robes billowing out around him in the blustery wind. He kept his mortarboard cap on his head with his free hand, and in the other he clutched the folder that held his hard-earned diploma.

Summa cum laude.

Well, that was over with. He climbed the steps to his fourth floor dorm room, taking a quick glance around the empty space, as if he'd forgotten to pack something. Not likely. Two paltry suitcases, a garbage bag of bedding, a coffee machine and a hot pot, and ten boxes of books. On the rare occasion fellow students came to visit, they always marveled at how he managed to live with so little. He would have laughed, but was afraid it would violate the terms of his non-disclosure agreement.

Even his monastic little dorm room seemed luxurious after living on the island.

He pulled the mortarboard off and tossed it on the bare mattress, sitting back in the wooden desk chair. The other graduates were probably still at the ceremony, taking snapshots with friends or planning celebratory meals with the families who'd come to see them walk across the stage and receive their diplomas.

The speeches had been nice, and Adam supposed, one day, he'd be glad he'd bothered to go to the ceremony. But today was not that day. He just felt tired. He'd spent the last three semesters doing the work of four, trying to make sure he was able to graduate on time with his class, despite his missing months. He'd worked his ass off making sure his graduate school applications were competitive with his classmates, and that his ambitions were still viable.

He'd dropped into bed every night only when he was sure exhaustion would carry him away to oblivion before he had a chance to think about *her*.

Kalina. It had been months until her picture had ceased gracing the covers of tabloid magazines at the supermarket, and a year before he didn't hear the echo of her name at every campus party. Adam had found it shockingly easy not to talk about her, even when everyone else was. If anyone asked him where he'd been all those months, he'd simply said, "family stuff" and folks left him alone.

Alone was better. It was real, at least. Adam had spent his childhood with people whose love was conditional, and five months with a woman whose love was a lie. It was better not to think that people ever cared than to get gut punched when you found out they never had.

He should really start hauling these boxes down to the car. He had an appointment to look at apartments in Georgetown tomorrow. There was no time like the present. Also, he should return his cap and gown, get back that deposit. He headed over to the bed to untangle his tassel from the cap. Another useless trinket. He should probably just toss it.

"Congratulations, Adam," came a voice at his back.

He stiffened, and the hairs on the nape of his neck rose. There was only one person in the world who sounded like that. Only one soul on Earth who could speak his name and make his heart stop in his chest.

"You looked really good up there," she went on, though he hadn't turned around. "I searched for you afterward, but it was a sea of black robes."

Finally, slowly, he turned, and stared at the vision filling his doorway.

Kalina looked different than he'd remembered. Healthier. Her cheeks were full instead of gaunt, and her breasts and hips were curvier. Her wild hair had been cut and styled into a sleek bob that grazed her shoulders. She wore a lavender top and a white skirt suit with a matching coat that swung around her knees. Her eye makeup was light, her lips pink and glossy.

And she was here.

"Of course," she added, "You know how I like a man in black." She entered the room, taking in the blank walls and the stacked boxes.

"Kalina," he said stupidly. His feet seemed rooted to the ground. He couldn't run away, but neither could he move toward her. She was in his room. He'd imagined it a hundred times, and expected it none.

"I was under the impression people sent graduation notices to their friends and families, but you never did."

He'd been paid not to. "I wasn't sure what we were."

"Friends?" she asked mildly, tugging open the flaps on the top book box. "Or family?"

"Neither."

She clucked her tongue. "You saved my life on that island, Adam. I saved yours. We spent months there, alone, together. We—"

"I know what we did," he ground out. "You don't have to remind me." What the hell was she doing here, other than torturing him with memories he'd spent a year trying to bury?

She gave him a long, silent look, then peeked at the spines in the box. "What's this?"

"Don't—" he said. "They're all packed—" Too late. She pulled out a battered paperback.

"*The Princess Bride*," she read aloud. "I thought I told you the movie was better."

"I don't like movies," Adam said. Lies. He'd liked that one. He'd borrowed the VHS and watched it at the student center. Lots. It wasn't quite as good as having Kalina act it out for him by firelight, but he'd take it.

He should kick her out. The contract he'd signed had been quite explicit. He was to have no further contact with Kalina St. Claire. But it hadn't said anything about what he should do when she barged into his dorm room. It hadn't said a word about how to make his hands stop tingling or chest stop aching.

They'd been right to post guards to keep him away from her last time. The only way he'd made it through this past year was knowing she was three states away…and didn't give a shit about him.

But then… what was she doing here?

She put the book back in the box and turned to him, looking uncertain. There was a large purse slung over her shoulder, and she played with the metal chain that served as its strap. "Are you glad to see me?"

Yes. His very cells seemed to turn toward her like a leaf toward sunlight. Was this a test?

"I'm glad to see that you are doing well."

And he hoped she'd go home. This wasn't good for his equilibrium. This wasn't good for his contract.

"I am doing well," she said. "I'm in school."

"That's great."

"Pre-med." She shrugged. "I'm kicking butt at it too. Turns out I'm quite smart. Or my tutors are very dedicated. Or maybe they're smart and I'm dedicated. At any rate, since I'm not taking any summers off, I have about a year of undergrad left—"

"What are you doing here?" Adam blurted out.

She blinked, taken aback. "I'm looking at Johns Hopkins. For med school."

"Wow," he said, unable to hold back his genuine reaction. "That's…amazing, Kalina. Really."

A doctor. He remembered the way she'd cared for him, back on the island. She'd known nothing, but she'd saved his life. It all made so much sense. And Hopkins was a top-notch program. Kalina must be doing very well, indeed. Either that or she'd written the school an enormous check. She did so like to write checks.

"Do you think so?" Her voice was soft and something in it gave him pause, made all his uncharitable thoughts melt away. For a second, he could pretend she really cared.

"You know I do," he said, defeated. Adam had no clue why she was standing in his room, but his defenses could only take so much. "I was your first patient. If that's what you want... I have no doubt that you can do whatever you put your mind to."

She stared at him for a long, silent moment, then cleared her throat and began digging inside her purse. "I thought I'd give you your graduation present."

"I think you've given me enough." The last thing he needed was some stupid card from the only woman he'd ever loved. Especially if it came with another check.

She was quiet for a moment, and her hands stilled. "I want you to know," she said at last, and there was a hitch in her voice he'd not expected, "that I was unaware of the contract you signed. And the money you were paid. That was entirely the work of a family lawyer no longer in my employ."

Adam's breath died in his chest. She sounded so formal, like someone who really did deserve being in control of the hundreds of millions of dollars her grandfather had left her. Yes, he occasionally read those tabloid headlines. The day he'd found out was the closest he'd come to breaking the terms of his contract and reaching out to her. Still, he hadn't. What kind of asshole called a girl who'd paid him off once already on the day when she inherited a fortune? Kalina had made her preference clear.

Or so he'd thought.

"Eric believed he was protecting me." She glanced up, and her eyes had gone red around the edges. "That's not an excuse, by the way. I fired him when I found out."

"But you still didn't call." The words came out as if someone else was saying them. For Adam would never say something like that. Could never. He was past it.

"Well," she said, and her shoulders hunched forward. "You took the money."

He went cold all over, like plunging into a shadowy pool. It had been eighteen months, and Kalina still had the power to destroy him with a sentence. He'd doomed them, and he'd never even known.

Yes, Adam took the money. And he wasn't going to give it back. "You have no idea, Kalina. You're from a different world."

"Yes. I know." She began to dig in her purse again, and pulled out a large manila envelope tied with a blue bow. "Here."

He stared at it like it was a bomb. "What to get for the boy who has nothing?"

The paper began to tremble and he dragged his eyes up to her face. She was holding her mouth tight, her chin high, but her eyes burned like twin flames.

"What are you doing here?" he asked again, his voice hardly equal to getting the words out. "I have to know."

"I grew up thinking I had everything," she said, and every word sounded like a gong. "But I was wrong. There were things I needed that I didn't find out about until too late. There were things I wanted that I never knew about at all. Now I know what I want, and I'll fight for it with everything I am."

But still, he was wary. "And what is that?"

She looked down at the envelope between them and said nothing. Adam took pity on her and took it out of her hands.

"Open it." She grimaced as the order slipped from her lips. "Please."

He didn't want to. He didn't want to see the new number, the new payoff, whatever she'd now decided he was worth for saving her life. But she'd asked, so he tore off the ribbon anyway.

A small sheaf of papers spilled out into his hand. An official looking document with some sort of strange seal. A satellite image, all blue but for a tiny speck. A deed.

A deed with his name on it. His name...and hers.

"I know I come from a different world," she said. "That's why I want a new one. A world we make together."

He raised his head and stared at her, his mouth open. "You bought the island?"

"Shockingly cheap," she replied, forcing a laugh. "You'd be amazed how little paradise can cost."

"I don't understand—" He looked at the papers again. *Dawnskeep Island.* It had a name. An actual name.

"The island was my new world," Kalina said. "I became who I am there. I hope it'll be our world, Adam. Because what I want is you."

It was as if the sun had broken through a cloud, shining rays of light right through him. This couldn't be real. He knew what was true: Kalina had abandoned him eighteen months ago. She'd given him fifty thousand dollars to disappear for good.

And yet she stood there, a few insignificant feet away, and she kept talking, and every word she spoke made the world glow bright.

"I know you came from the middle of nowhere, and so I understand why this proposal might totally freak you out—"

"Proposal?"

She blushed. "I mean..." She stopped, and her hands fisted at her side as she lifted her chin in defiance. "Yes. That's what I mean. That's what I'm here for, Adam. You and me and the life I want us to make together."

There was no angle in her words, no artifice, no armor. She stood before him and laid her soul bare. He held her heart in his hands, and it was shaped like a desert island.

"I've never been proposed to before," he found himself saying.

Relief flashed across her face, along with the tiniest of smiles. "I have. Do you want some tips?"

"Sure."

She took a deep breath. "Make sure the person doing the proposing wants everything about you, everything you are and could possibly hope to become. And make sure that they are offering you the same of themselves. That was the problem I ran into when I used to get proposed to all the time. No one even knew who I was, let alone believed in all the things I wanted to be."

"And now?"

"In this case, everything is in place."

How could it be? He wanted to go to graduate school. She'd just finished telling him she was planning on becoming a doctor. And she bought them an island. Adam looked down at the map in his hands. *Their* island. Their lonely, distant island. Their private, perfect island.

Was this what she wanted? To go back to the island? "I can't spend my life hiding away." That's what his parents had done. They'd hidden away and told him only about the worst parts of humanity. He'd never be like them.

"I don't want you to. It's a base, a start, a new dawn. I would never want you to turn your back on the world. I don't want to either."

"Then what is this?"

"It's our safe place. Yours and mine. And... our children's. The world tried to ruin me, Adam, but I still want to save it. I know we have years of school ahead of us—both of us. But we also have years of building before this island can become any kind of home. I want it there for us, always, to remind us of what we can be."

Dawnskeep Island. *She* had named it. The papers spilled from his hands and he took two steps forward, straight to Kalina. Her hair felt like silk beneath his fingertips, her skin warm and soft. He cupped her head in his hands and his lips hovered over hers. This would never do—Kalina proposing in an empty dorm room while he wore his graduation robes. She was Kalina St. Claire. She deserved champagne and fire-swallowers and diamonds the size of teacups. This would never work out.

Oh, hell. Who cared?

"Marry me," she insisted. "I love you."

"I love you, too," he said. "And I swear I will spend my life making you happy, whether it's here or Dawnskeep or the surface of the moon." He kissed her then, a deep and lasting kiss, filled with the longing of the last eighteen months, and the promise of the next eighty years.

"And I will make sure you are everything you want to be," Kalina said, when at last he pulled away. "You and I both. Bring me back to our island, Adam, and I know together we can conquer the world."

As he gathered her close, Adam knew there was only one thing he could say.

"As you wish."

author's note

I'd like to extend my thanks to beta readers K.A. Linde and Jessica Carnes, as well as Carrie Ryan for brainstorming, and Jen Barnes for helping me indulge my id. Thanks also to Heidi Joy Tretheway, who has helped so much in every aspect of production, as well as hand holding.

A hundred nights in paradise to my amazing cover photographer, Vania Stoyanova, who perfectly captured the beauty and heat of… um, Dawnskeep Island. Yeah, the island.

Thank you, thank you, thank you to Lisa Christman, my angel editor. You're totally right about the koopas.

Heartfelt gratitude to everyone involved with either the book or the film *The Princess Bride*. Each are perfect in their own inimitable way, which is why Kalina loves you so much. For all *The Princess Bride* fans, I hoped you enjoyed hunting all the Easter eggs I've hidden in this story, and for those of you who haven't seen it yet—what are you waiting for?

And finally, thank you, reader. I hope you enjoyed this retro trip.

Kalina and Adam may have found their happily-ever-after, but the story of Dawnskeep Island is far from over. Pre-order *Island Born* today, and turn the page for a sneak peek at the first chapter.

Other Books by Viv Daniels

One & Only (Canton, #1)
HearMe

The Island Series (Coming Soon)
Island Born (#1)
Island Affair (#2)
Island Lost (#3)
Island's End (#4)

http://vivdaniels.com

ISLAND BORN

one

Dawnskeep Island
Coral Sea
October 5, 2014

Dear Sir William,

I was very happy to receive the invitation you forwarded from the professor. Her social experiment sounds interesting, if a bit far-fetched, and I'm pleased to say I'm free to participate in it. I doubt there are any "long term deleterious" effects from my parents' unconventional choices regarding my upbringing, but I am more than happy to help demonstrate as much, especially as this project seems to come with so many perks.

It has long been a wish of mine to visit the rest of the world and learn more about the places that, since I was a small child, I have only seen in books. After giving it some thought, I have decided we need not inform my parents. After all, they are abroad for the season on separate missions, and they have always in the past welcomed visitors to Dawnskeep.

Please inform Dr. Enoch that I am happy to move forward with the project, provided that she adhere to my preferred time schedule, and a few other particulars, detailed on the attached sheet. As our family attorney, you will of course already attend to the standard Dawnskeep contractual requirements. Though this contract will be in my name rather than my parents', I feel it is best to stick with what has worked in the past.

And again, I thank you for your continued discretion.

Sincerely,

Joshua St. Claire Truman

For the hundredth time, Carrie Young lifted the envelope to her nose and inhaled. It was impossible, she knew, but the hand-folded paper smelled of the sea. Smelled of hot tropical nights, of monsoons and endless blue water and atolls and the man who'd sent the aroma from half a world away.

She looked up and caught another woman staring at her from across the terminal lounge. Quickly, she placed the envelope back its appropriate file and stuffed them both inside her briefcase.

"Love letter?" the woman asked.

Not quite, though she sure did love the letter. She practically had it memorized. Carrie shook her head and smiled sheepishly.

"Thought not. Never heard of a man spritzing his letters with cologne."

Carrie nodded absently, her gaze straying once again to the briefcase. She couldn't stop touching the letter, couldn't stop examining it from every angle like an investigator looking for clues. The strange, uneven font that spoke of manual typewriters and damp paper, the precise, old-fashioned syntax, the firm loops of the writer's signature. Joshua St. Claire Truman.

Besides, it was her job to observe him, wasn't it? To notice every nuance of his behavior, to mark down the changes and watch for signs that would show that Dr. Enoch's hypothesis was correct.

Still, she should be careful not to go overboard. She didn't want to do anything off-base in front of the professor. Not when she was so close to her goal.

The South Pacific. For three months. The journey was a research assistant's dream, a coup from which the entire department – some more experienced, all more polished and definitely more knowledgeable – had yet to recover. Carrie had gleefully undergone the perfunctory physical, endured all the shots and vaccinations required for a trip to the edge of civilization. She'd submitted herself to the barrage of personality tests that questioned her ability to perform the unique tasks required by the nature of the project. She'd studied for months to appear proficient in Dr. Blevin's work in developmental psychology. She didn't want her new boss to have a moment's doubt about Carrie's ability to perform up to expectations.

After all, the famous scientist had made Carrie's dreams come true. The least she could do as her research assistant would be to return the favor.

Carrie found herself grinning, a new habit she just couldn't seem to lick.

"It *is* a love letter," said the persistent woman in the opposite chair.

"No," Carrie replied, smiling openly now. "It's a new job. I'm going to the south Pacific on a research trip." *And I can't wait.*

"Oh," she said. "Are you a scientist?"

"Yes," Carrie replied. *I guess I am.* Unreal. A few short years ago she'd never thought she could answer a question like that. She was nothing. Nobody.

I'm the only one who will ever want you.

Carrie squeezed her eyes and banished Darrin's voice into a far corner of her brain, where it belonged. That life was behind her. That person wasn't someone she would even recognize anymore. Carrie Young was a straight-A student with a full scholarship and promising future.

She repeated it to herself several times in a row, until her heartbeat slowed into an acceptable range.

"I'm Allison," the woman across the way said. "What's your name?"

Carrie looked at the blanks screen of her phone and pretended to look annoyed. "I'm sorry, I have to take this." She pressed it to her ear and stood up, dragging her rolling suitcase behind her as she pretended to speak to someone.

It was ridiculous, really. Darrin had not hired this woman to nab her outside the gate of a plane to Fiji. But old habits died hard, and she'd be self-conscious until she was safely out of the country. Maybe she should have bought a wig, just in case.

No, Carrie. Shut up. It's been four years. Four years since she'd heard anything from Darrin. If he'd wanted to come looking for her, he'd have done so already.

Still, Carrie didn't come out of the bathroom until she heard her flight called to board. On the plane, she checked her own number twice.

"Excuse me," she said to the flight attendant. "I think there's some mistake. I'm not flying first class."

The flight attendant glanced at her ticket, then up at Carrie, a pitying smile flashing across her face. "This is business class. Can I bring you anything? Champagne?"

She looked at the space in front of her. This wasn't an airline seat, but some sort of enormous couch inside its own cubicle. "I—"

"Don't worry," the stewardess went on. "It's complimentary."

In the seat, Carrie opened the folder Dr. Enoch had mailed to her last week. First class—or business class, rather—surely that wasn't included in the university's grant. She went over the travel arrangements again, and everything looked the same. Coach class tickets, taxi to the docks where she'd meet Dr. Enoch and the other research assistants for the last leg of the journey, by boat, out to Dawnskeep Island.

The flight attended returned with a split of champagne and a crystal glass. "I checked the computer, and you got an upgrade," she informed Carrie as she poured. "Looks like this is your lucky day."

Carrie wasn't used to lucky days. Then again, wasn't that this entire voyage? One giant, unbelievable stroke of luck?

"If I were you, hon, I'd enjoy it." The attendant patted the luxurious head cushion and moved on.

Carrie put her feet up on the rest, leaned into the reclining backrest, and took a sip of her champagne. Enjoy it, huh? She could try.

The folder still sat in her lap, fat with information about their subject and his family history, and as the champagne bubbled through her system and the flight took off into the blue January sky, she flipped it open again.

Name: *Joshua St. Claire Truman*
DOB: *December 31, 1993*
Parents: *Drs. Adam Truman and Kalina St. Claire Truman*
Siblings: *Aurora Elizabeth (13), Charles William (5)*

Twenty-one years old, and probably painfully naive. Joshua Truman had been raised in nearly total isolation, alone on a tropical island his parents had bought for the express purpose of keeping their children guarded from the world.

Also in the folder were printouts of a profile *Time* magazine had once done on the St. Claire Trumans. There were pictures of the glamorous mother, an heiress and former socialite with a vast fortune and a taste for philanthropy. After receiving her medical degree, Kalina St. Claire Truman had devoted her life to building field hospitals in Pakistan, Indonesia, Cambodia, and central Africa. Carrie paused on one picture of the woman, her pretty dark hair wrapped up in a colorful scarf, playing on the floor of a hut with a group of skinny African orphans. At her knee was a chubby little white boy with big eyes, pouting into the camera like it was intruding on their game.

Joshua. This must have been before they'd moved him to the island permanently. Even then, he seemed distrustful of outsiders, of the media that was wild to scrutinize every aspect of his famous mother's life.

Carrie vaguely remembered the story, the way you remember Princess Di was killed by paparazzi in a high speed chase. Kalina St. Claire had been shipwrecked on a desert island, and when she came home, she was never quite the same. She used to date Wall Street guys and rock stars, but then she became a doctor, married some professor no one had ever heard of, and bought the very island instrumental in her survival.

Dawnskeep Island.

Carrie supposed a shipwreck might make anyone a little crazy. And with Dr. Truman's work in the poorest and most dangerous of countries, maybe it made sense that she'd want to protect her children from the ills of the world.

But, as Dr. Enoch had said, every choice came with a price. The price a human paid for such social isolation... it was one Carrie understood more than she'd ever admit.

When she read Joshua's letter, beneath the formal diction and the carefully worded demands, she sensed fear. He was terrified his parents would discover that he'd gone behind their back to invite visitors to Dawnskeep, that he was planning to leave without their knowledge.

She'd asked Dr. Enoch, during the planning stages, if she believed his parents were holding him there against his will.

"Please, Miss Young," the professor had scoffed. "I'm far more concerned that the boy will experience a nervous breakdown the second we get to Tokyo. Remember, his socialization has been entirely stunted by his bizarre rearing. Did you read that book I gave you on feral child case studies?"

She had, but the man who had written that letter was not a feral child. Was not a child at all, though Dr. Enoch always referred to him as a boy. When Carrie had questioned her on the designation, she'd waved it off.

"You will see when you meet him," she'd said. "No one who has been raised as he has could possibly have grown into an normal, functioning adult."

Carrie scanned the rest of the file. Joshua Truman could speak five languages, played three instruments—not named—and held an international baccalaureate diploma. There was nothing wrong with his intellect, at least.

And yet, he was twenty-one years old and hadn't left the island home his parents had built for him since he'd been thirteen. At the very least, there was a mystery here, and Dr. Enoch and her team were eager to solve it.

As Carrie finished her champagne, she searched the file again, as though it might contain a previously overlooked clue. Of course, there was nothing. Carrie had the info practically memorized. She knew what they all knew—Joshua's family history and education—and what they didn't. He'd never had a psychological work up. They didn't even have a recent photo.

Just the letter. Carrie peeked around but everyone up here in business class was buried in their own work, in their own little comfort pod. She examined the letter again. Perfectly typed. Who knew how to actually type anymore? Had Joshua ever seen a computer? Did he know what social media was?

Well, that at least, they had in common. Carrie's friends always wondered why she wasn't on Facebook, why they had no account to tag in pictures on Instagram. But she couldn't risk Darrin finding her pictures online.

Still, she'd made that choice herself. Joshua's parents seemed to have made it for him. And if she read between the lines of his letter, he had decided it was time for a change.

Carrie looked out the window as the sun turned the surface of the ocean to molten gold, and raised a glass to him, somewhere out there in the endless sea.

From one escapee to another, cheers.